PACHYDERM

A Catherine Kint Mystery

HUGH MCGINLAY

Clan Destine
PRESS

This edition published by Clan Destine Press in 2021
  First published by Threekookaburras 2017

Clan Destine Press
PO Box 121, Bittern
Victoria, 3918 Australia

National Library of Australia Cataloguing-In-Publication data:

McGinlay, Hugh

Pachyderm

ISBN: 978-0-6450021-5-7 (paperback)
ISBN: 978-0-6450021-3-3 (eBook)

Cover Design by © Willsin Rowe
Design & Typesetting by Clan Destine Press

Clan Destine
P R E S S

www.clandestinepress.net

For Patrick Northey,
who taught me a great deal about elephants

1

If they made liquor out of damp grass, it would smell a bit like that.
~ Beau Hacska

'I didn't really have perspective on life until my head got stuck inside an elephant's anal tract.'

It wasn't the worst line Catherine had heard that night, which in itself was remarkable. An unexpected line on a surprise night out in a location that would have been beautiful even without free champagne. Had it been said elsewhere it would have died a quick and painful death, yet tonight it worked.

Of course, the delivery helped the line, as did the champagne, as did the deliverer who was tall, dark-haired and well versed in all things zoological. Five minutes after meeting her, Beau had taken a champagne bottle and led her from the party to see the moon rise over the gorilla cages in a zoo just north of Melbourne.

Beau had a way of saying amazing things and not seeming like he was showing off. His handsome face and sleepy eyes were lovely and Catherine had to admit she liked his voice, his laugh and his tight zoo-keeper pants. Also the way he walked easily through the crowd of tuxedos to take a bottle whilst wearing said zoo-keeper pants. Sometimes, it's in a man's walk.

Confident gait aside, there's always the moonlight to add an extra layer of enticement. As a flatterer, moonlight is the ultimate and most ancient visual aphrodisiac. It doesn't take a genius to realise that phrases like "the cold light of day" – Catherine was aware of equivalents on at least three continents – came from the removal of that satellite's soft, silvery illumination.

Perhaps it was five million years of humanity looking at the pale reflected light that made wrinkles fade, eyes glow and features soften, that made us one of the few species that – although mostly day-dwelling – are nocturnal in our mating rituals. Tonight, that light had travelled 150 million-odd kilometres to reach Beau's face. Catherine decided it had been worth the trip. She went back to listening to his voice.

'It's just a reference point, one of those things you wake up to. First thoughts of the day: I'm alive, I'm tired, that alarm is loud, I probably won't have my head up an elephant's anal tract today. It really starts the day with a kick.'

'And you can imagine how happy the elephant is on such mornings.' As he laughed, Catherine took a long drink of champagne and moved a few elegant dance steps on the zoo's sandy path. She had enjoyed a haircut today and was aware of her severe bob framing her face, rounded out with a silver pillbox adorned with an asymmetric swirl doubling back on itself. A boorish man with a Dutch accent and a double-barrelled name had earlier in the evening commented on her 'delectable chocolatey eyes'. By comparison, Beau's discussion on an elephant's colon was well above par.

Beau rubbed the back of his neck as they walked, glancing upwards at the bamboo that lined both sides of the path. 'Chung-de was at least twice as traumatised as I was.'

'I remember the footage. I saw it on the news.'

'It played here, too?'

'After the weather,' she said. 'A slice of life story about the pitfalls of getting too involved in your work. Footage from Berlin Zoo. They didn't mention you were Australian.'

'I was quite happy to remain anonymous.'

'True, your face was well hidden.'

They came to a small clearing near a large enclosure. Beau climbed a large rock he had chosen as their vantage point and offered Catherine a hand up.

'Yeah, I didn't believe in fifteen minutes of fame. It's quite an experience.'

Catherine adjusted her pillbox for a better rock ascending angle. 'You're the most famous zoo-keeper here.'

She climbed up to join him, ignoring his offered hand. A moment later they were seated atop the rock, watching the yellow gibbous moon slowly escaping the horizon.

'I thought you might have mentioned Bradbury.'

'The living legend?'

'Oh God, who said that?' Even in the moonlight she could see Beau's face wrinkle. Even when he snorted he looked attractive.

'Our gracious host, when she introduced me to him.' Catherine found the champagne and busily filled her glass.

'I didn't think he would give himself that title.'

'I didn't recognise him at first, though he must have been on television for most of my life.' Catherine leaned into Beau, finding his shoulder quite comfortable. She silently toasted her millinery client, the wonderful, high maintenance Diana, who was so delighted with her broad brim hat that she rewarded Catherine with a ticket to the opening.

Below them, the gorilla enclosure was quiet; of Otana and his hominid company, there was no sign. After being quiet for half a minute, Beau kissed her. Catherine had wondered about more small talk, but he had obviously decided to get it out of the way. He smelled like the outside, like grass and rock, like soil and sweat, tasted like champagne and felt like fun. She was glad she hadn't walked away when she realised Grace was the keynote speaker.

Grace was serious, blonde and beautiful. She had a sheen of success clinging to her designer corporate clothes. Even if you didn't know she was a cabinet minister at a ridiculously young age, you'd have guessed. Grace Chichester was a political tour de force with a razor sharp intellect, naked ambition and an influential family name. She used her assets to cut through traditions of age and gender with seeming ease. Like many who knew her, Catherine had followed her career, been appalled at her policies and never, ever forgotten their past. Tonight, just the sight of her had been enough to remember their first encounter.

Grace Chichester had been the first girl Catherine had been paired with at Chiefly Girls Grammar. A young Catherine, laden down with books and parental expectation, had followed Grace towards the Year Seven quarters, Grace checking her plaits for consistency as they walked. Grace immediately wanted to know where she had "summered". Catherine replied she had been in Cambodia, volunteering in an orphanage with her father. Grace had jumped back in horror and laughed loudly. When Catherine asked what she was doing, Grace replied she was staying clear of fleas.

The relationship hadn't improved with time. Grace had called her "Nurnur" forever, "Nur" being code for NR – Nouveau Riche. Over the years they had at times pulled hair and kicked, when Catherine's karate came in most handy. Then, from around age fifteen, it got worse. Catherine became invisible to Grace. This shouldn't have annoyed Catherine, but did. There are few things so irritating in life as having a nemesis who has forgotten you.

At the opening of the zoo's new meerkat enclosure, Catherine's walk through the beautiful leafy gardens had soured upon sight of her old enemy. The Right Honourable Grace Chichester MP was looking down her surgically altered nose – Catherine was sure – when Grace saw her. The Minister for Parks and Environment gave a contemptuous glance towards her old classmate. Catherine's shoulders did not slump and she smiled a perfectly agreeable smile at Grace, though she instantly wanted to check her teeth, armpits and grenade stockpile.

Grace looked well and every inch the parliamentarian. Her features were serious, presumably from the business of keeping Planet Earth turning for the ignorant masses. Catherine noted Grace was between her and the drinks table, speaking quietly and earnestly to the Lord Mayor. Grace moved away as Catherine came near.

'Catherine, how are you?' Her chin came up by several degrees.

Catherine smiled, and felt suddenly drunk. 'Very well, your membership.'

Grace smiled and exhaled slightly, as if disappointed. Her eyes flicked almost imperceptibly as she judged her audience. 'I knew it was you. I recognise your style of hat – no one but you would wear it.'

Catherine edged around her; the champagne was close. 'Don't worry Grace, most of the world are still conformists.'

'Most people work, too.'

Catherine, eyes twitching, studiously not rising to the bait. 'How is Parliament?'

Her eyes widened along with her grin. She spoke low. 'It's harder work than some could do. But it keeps me busy.'

Catherine wondered how long she'd wanted to say that. 'Each serves as best they can, that was your Dad's big thing wasn't it?'

'Legacy is a difficult template, Nurnur,' Grace replied with a smile.

Catherine thought of how much she hated her.

'Though not everyone is so keen to fulfil their potential, are they?'

Catherine rolled her eyes in response.

'Sorry Grace, I've found champagne.'

'I'm sure you do that regularly.'

Catherine moved away and accepted a glass from the white-clad drinks attendant. She felt a hand on her shoulder and turned to see her client, Diana, who had invited her to the event, and her host, Georgia Potter, chairwoman of the zoo board. With her was a man in his mid-sixties with a face so familiar Catherine wondered if he was a family friend she hadn't seen for some years.

'Hello, it's Catherine, isn't it? Have you had a chance to meet Ian?' Georgia's bespectacled face was beaming, either with champagne, benevolence or proximity to celebrity. Ian became recognisable – his was the face of a thousand documentaries.

He held out his hand. 'Ian Bradbury.'

'Of course, I've seen you for years on television.'

He gave a small smile, easy with the compliment.

'I was just complimenting Diana on that fabulous hat. Georgia pointed you out. I wanted to say hello.' He had a thick Yorkshire accent.

Catherine smiled while she calculated how many years older he was than her own father. 'Lovely to meet you. I think the last show I saw was about tigers.'

His face lit up. 'Sumatrans? Yes. I enjoyed filming that, must be seven years ago. Their numbers are so low now that genetically they're in grave danger.'

He shook his head ruefully, swaying a little.

'Inbred tigers, toothless?'

He laughed, the zoo's chairwoman joining him a millisecond afterwards. Catherine thought he could pull off a bowler, as men of a certain age could do. If he started wearing one of hers it would really boost her sales to men.

'What are you working on now?' Catherine's glass was getting dangerously low.

'Ian is working with us here in our carnivore and trail sections. It's a real coup for the zoo,' Georgia enthused.

'I like working with animals, even without a camera in my face,' Ian told her. He leaned closer. 'How do you fill your days?'

A manicured hand split their faces. 'She wastes them. Hello, Ian.'

Bradbury's face lit up in a way Catherine had previously only seen in television advertisements for his programs. 'Grace, how lovely. Do you know Catherine?'

'For years,' Grace said, without breaking eye contact with Ian. Her shoulder was now practically blocking his face from Catherine's. 'Tell me, how are you settling into your pad?'

Georgia looked bashful as Catherine backed away, amazed at the sensation of gratitude towards Grace. She steadied herself with a champagne and the knowledge of Grace's poor intentions.

It was about then Beau winked at her. She smiled back, admiring his zoo-keeper uniform. He approached her, a khaki clad gentleman in a courtyard of penguins.

He nodded towards Grace. 'I had an experience like that once, can I tell you about it?'

In the distance, an elephant called. Beau's shoulder became rigid for a second, then relaxed as they continued canoodling. He was becoming more ardent and Catherine was wondering how far a lady went in such close proximity to a gorilla enclosure. While much of her consciousness was in the moment, her cerebral self was coming to the following conclusions: it's a case-by-case basis – one must check the reasons why. If it's simply to notch up the experience of having bonked near our evolutionary cousin, then it's a bad idea. If it's a spiritual, emotionally mature interaction with someone who possesses amazing pectoral muscles and is a welcome distraction from Grace, then it's a no-brainer.

A static, muffled voice squawked from Beau's waistline. 'Beau. Where the hell are you? Dong Zei's having a fit.'

Beau broke contact and blinked as his eyes came back into focus. He fumbled for the walkie-talkie on his belt. 'I hear you Simon, coming.'

He leapt from the rock, pausing to look at Catherine.

'Sorry. Sick elephant.' He gave a half smile, half wince.

Catherine reached for the quarter-full champagne bottle, and gave a wink that was lost in the darkness. 'Happens all the time.'

'To be continued,' Beau called out over his shoulder as he jogged towards the elephants.

'Indeed.' Catherine poured the remainder into her glass and toasted the sleeping hominids. The champagne was lovely, even tastier for being warmed a little. Without thinking, she jumped from the rock without spilling a drop, though she did hop twice to avoid twisting her ankle. As she walked through the bamboo, a growing throng of zoo staff and guests moved towards the elephant enclosure.

Catherine joined them and saw a strange mirroring of elephant and human society. All that was visible of the elephants were backsides as the herd of five looked inside the inner and hidden part of their enclosure, where calls came from a distressed elephant, pain and fear having similar sounds across the species. The humans followed suit, staring at something they could not see. Catherine noted one staff member was keeping a close eye on the guests, lest they jump the fence to give inter-species mouth to mouth. Catherine was glad Boris wasn't there.

Realising that global warming had again caused her champagne to evaporate, she decided that she would best serve the stricken elephant by leaving it to the experts. She began the trek back to the function for the promise of more champagne while she waited for Beau.

Her pace slowed imperceptibly as she noted Grace was again between her and the bar, speaking airily with three women Catherine found hauntingly familiar. Catherine's hand immediately went to her hair, smoothing any ruffles on her bob. She remembered the women's faces but not names, which, for a woman of her memory, must have taken some effort. Grace smiled brilliantly.

'Is the elephant okay?'

Catherine slowed but did not stop. 'The diagnosis is unclear, but it's in the hands of experts.'

Grace smiled like an evil Grace Kelly. 'It's not the only one.'

The three little maids from school tittered like teenagers. The fact that they were all thirty made it gross and turned Catherine's stomach.

'One has to find excitement in these times of drudgery.' Catherine found a bottle and poured, generously.

One of the sidekicks spoke up. 'He didn't seem too dull.'

'I was just quoting something he said earlier.'

Catherine thought she saw a scowl for a second but by the time she looked up Grace was again beaming. 'So glad you were able to brighten his evening. A great use of your talents.'

She turned to an offsider. 'Candace, could Catherine help solve that issue of the speech to the old school about creativity?'

Catherine's gut fell as Candace agreed. Speaking at the old school would be enough for her to want to shout the bar a round, or even call her mother. It was ego, pride, it shouldn't matter, but it did.

Grace continued, 'I've been asked, you see, and I haven't the time. I could put in a word to the vice-principal.'

Catherine put a hand to her hat. 'Don't put yourself out, Grace.'

'Oh, Catherine, I didn't mean you. I wondered if you perhaps had Serena Lindeman's contact details? The fees are high. Let's show the kids some success stories, right?'

Catherine fought the urge to slap her and walked away. Thankfully for her ego, she soon found another woman wearing one of her hats. For the next fifteen minutes they chatted about the colours for next racing season and she took Catherine's card. Another fruitful night for the office.

People started coming back to the party but the looks on their faces told Catherine the news wasn't good. A pale-faced woman shook her head slowly. 'It died. Someone said it could be a heart attack. The keepers are up there. One of them is crying.'

Catherine could hear more elephant calls. Suddenly the party was tapering off. Catherine toyed with the idea of waiting for Beau, but decided against it. If he were the keeper crying, he wouldn't want her to see and if he wasn't, he'd be holding the others up. He seemed like the type.

Picking up her bag she placed a hand on the shoulder of her host, Georgia Potter, who stood farewelling revellers as they shuffled out. Grace was holding court behind her, discussing the importance of a super road to connect the eastern and western suburbs, even if it meant moving the zoo. Georgia left the group at that point. As she moved away, Catherine could hear the squawk of an imperious bird.

2

Things taste better with sacrifice.

~ Boris Shakhovskoy

Over the general hubbub an anguished cry rang out. Catherine turned back to the party with other guests who had been leaving as the wailing became louder. She thought it was an animal, until a tuxedoed man marched around the drinks table. He had a thin build, but it was hard to be sure until he was in the lights of the party. He was stumbling, but made quick progress towards Georgia Potter. His cries rose in a crescendo as he screamed, 'Murder! Murder! Murder!'

He was near the zoo's director, his arms striking the air, shrieking, 'Murder, murder, your keeper!'

A security guard walked towards him. He lurched away but quickly corrected himself as drunks do around the globe. His face was distorted by rage, eyes wild and glazed and his mouth a loose snarl as he stumbled towards her. Catherine suspected he didn't drink often but had had a heroic dose of champagne.

He stopped in front of Georgia. 'On your watch, this magnificent creature is gone because of his incompetence!'

Georgia remained poised though her face was pale. Catherine heard the words, "poison", "incompetence" and "trial" before he raised his arm as though to strike Georgia.

Catherine ran towards him, her eyes fixed on his hand which was stable, but for how long? She counted the steps as she propelled towards him: one two, three four. Her view of the man was suddenly blocked by a body, who pulled him easily away. Catherine finished sprinting and tried to look casual, aware that she in fact looked ridiculous.

Her aborted dash led her to Georgia, who looked stunned as the two men, one her attacker and one her saviour, moved away. Catherine turned to see who had subdued the man and saw Ian Bradbury walking away, an arm around him.

Catherine moved her head to catch the light. 'You know him?'

Georgia watched them go; a hand went to her head and removed her glasses. 'I thought I did.'

'Staff?'

Georgia nodded in a half present sort of way.

'Are you all right?' Catherine asked, touching her arm.

'I'm sure he wouldn't have hurt me.'

She paused, looking at Catherine's feet, then her face and back again. 'I've never known him to, hmm,' that was all Georgia could force from the sentence. She tried to laugh, failed. Then said 'hmm' again.

Catherine decided the poor woman had had enough excitement.

'Thanks for a lovely evening.'

As she walked away she saw the man, fifty metres away, being spoken to urgently by Ian Bradbury. Catherine adjusted her pillbox as she went into the night.

Eight minutes later, the Upfield train groaned into Royal Park Station, and Catherine boarded. The carriage was not full, though not empty of sound. As she looked for a seat Catherine heard whistling.

Conspicuous behaviour in the confines of public transport is particularly discouraged for anyone over the age of four. Catherine saw this as a throwback to the British roots of Australian colonisation. This had always been of great disappointment to Catherine, who enjoyed the chatter of life around her in the trains of less uptight corners of the earth.

The whistler was a bearded man of light complexion and brown hair, lighter than her own, wearing a black suit that made Catherine wonder if he had come from the same party. Tall and lean, he slouched against the doors with his head tilted back and his eyes closed. Catherine noticed two things: first, he would pull off a tam o'shanter; second, he was clearly happy.

As they headed towards Jewel Station, Catherine picked the tune as

Bonnie Tyler's *Total Eclipse of the Heart*. After resisting for ten seconds the mood took her and she puckered up and joined him, providing a perfect harmony into the chorus. The man's eyes opened and his cheek flexed with the pressure of attempting to keep whistling while smiling.

Humans will one day evolve to the point where either they can smile and whistle at the same time, or not find whistling in unison ridiculously funny. Currently only five per cent of the global population can pull this off, and Catherine's duet partner seemed to be one of the chosen few. To add difficulty to enjoyment, Catherine held onto a pole and made some impromptu stage moves.

From Brunswick Station onward they kept their eyes locked as they achieved an impromptu *puccalo* and forever was going to start tonight. As Anstey Station flashed into view Catherine, with dramatic slowness, let go of the pole and shuffled back towards the doors. The male whistler bowed slightly and a group of students gave a spontaneous round of applause as she stepped on to the platform. As the doors closed, she spread her fingers in a wave and gave the song one more chorus, watching as the train sped from view. There is nothing better than a surprise song, even a whistled one.

Catherine was heading for home when a voice within her cried out 'turn around bright eyes' and she did, to walk to the public drinking house known as the Glasgow Palace.

Her phone rang, private number.

'This is Catherine.'

'Hi. It's me.' Beau's voice. It seemed he moved fast. Only three hours into knowing him and he was a "me".

'Hi, me,' Catherine's tone went low, 'how are you holding up?'

'I'm better than some of the others. It's quite shit, really.'

'Was it expected?'

'She was given a clean bill of health two days ago.'

Catherine winced, the sound of her boot heels on the pavement reminding her of a heartbeat. 'Sorry.'

Beau chuckled. 'No, I'm sorry,' he said, 'I was ringing to apologise for running off, not garner sympathy.'

'You've the best vocab of anyone I've ever met whose head has been up an elephant's arse.'

He laughed. She continued, 'I live in Brunswick, if you need a place to be.'

'Oh, thanks.' He paused, considering. 'Not tonight. Believe it or not, there's some thought that I missed something when I gave her a clean bill of health. So I have to get my house in order and fight for my job.'

He paused. 'I appreciate the thought. Any other night.'

Catherine shivered and wondered if it were a reflex to being turned down. 'Didn't seem the time to be seemly.'

Beau's tone was somewhere between playful and earnest. 'I'm free tomorrow after work.'

'Call me at four. Let's find out if seemliness is still on holiday.'

With that, Catherine rang off and entered the pub. The room fanned out before her, wide and dotted with drinkers basking in the light of tea candles and dim lights. She moved between the faux dark wood tables to the bar and found herself in the presence of her two favourite things. A large gin and tonic, and the hirsute form of Boris Seamus Shakhovskoy. Barman, muscle and raconteur.

Boris winked as he accepted her credit card for its usual position in the tab book. 'How was the night, boss?'

'An elephant died, I got a smooch on a rock, Grace is still the biggest pain on this planet and believe it or not someone refused a night of passion with me. You?'

Boris stroked his beard as he considered it. 'Jimmy burnt my parma, but then gave me extra chips. I'm even-steven.'

'Glad to hear it. Got any peanuts?' Catherine looked down the length of the bar.

'You in mourning for the elephant?'

'Somewhat sentimental, so, yes.'

Boris poured some Nobbies into a brown bowl before he was called away to serve a pint.

Catherine rolled a peanut between her fingers and thought of the moon over the gorilla cage. It had been a little while since a smooch like that. Aside from a short tryst with an Israeli model it had, thus far, been a year of celibacy. Still, she reflected, life wasn't meant to be a production line of lovers, or moments such as a snog near an animal enclosure would be rendered meaningless. Catherine popped a peanut and sipped the gin as Boris came back, rubbing a wineglass with a tea towel.

'Did you say you were rejected?'

'Yes, indeed, though I think postponed is probably both better for my ego and closer to the truth.'

Boris nodded, multi-tasking while he restocked the crisp packets. 'I have no doubt of your allure. What was Grace up to?'

'Kissing babies and being a pretentious, joyless harridan. Thankfully, I missed the keynote speech by picking up a zoologist named Beau.'

Boris dropped a pack of salt and vinegar, and looked thoughtful as he picked it up. 'Beau Hacska?'

Catherine's face was blank. 'I've no idea, it was cut short by a dying elephant.'

'Beau Hacska is the guy who had his head stuck in an elephant's–'

Catherine's gin stopped halfway to her mouth. 'My dear Boris, how on earth would you know that?'

'I read an article about him transferring back to Australia from Germany.'

Catherine was suddenly conscious of keeping her voice down. 'Well, yes, he did mention it.'

The sides of Boris' lips began a dangerous upturn. 'Wasn't his pick-up line, was it?'

Catherine ate a peanut and was suddenly very interested in a tram passing outside. A few minutes later Leon, the publican, gave Boris a talking to about lying on the floor of the bar laughing. Wiping tears, Boris returned to his post while Leon began putting the chairs up. Last drinks had been called. Boris was suddenly in a rare mood.

'Oh, that's great. You smooched a bloke who smooched an elephant's intestine and you did it in full knowledge. No wonder Grace was getting your goat.'

'It's possibly not the kind of thing I would want in the alma mater magazine.'

She cleared her throat. 'He's very charming Boris, he knows a great number of collective nouns. Did you know a group of hippopotami are referred to as a bloat?'

Boris went serious and he placed his palms down on the bar. 'One, I'm sure I read about the collective noun stuff in *How to pick up chicks* and two, how about hippopotamuses?'

Catherine casually pushed her empty glass into his hand as she answered. 'Two, both are considered the accepted plural. And one, get stuffed. If you saw his biceps and how he looked in his pants you would know he's never read a dating book in his life.'

'Well, me neither, when it comes to it. Sadly, that crap has become part of the collective unconscious.' He took the glass and moved towards the dishwasher.

Catherine picked up her bag. 'I suppose I should be leaving.'

'Give me five to shut the tills and I'll come with you.'

Catherine lingered, unconvincingly checking her watch. 'I could be busy.'

Boris snorted. 'I know you've been rejected by captain elephant tract. You need support.'

He looked at her earnestly, and she shrugged.

Two hours later Boris was ensconced on his favourite spot on earth, Catherine's couch. He had three empty stubbies in front of him on the coffee table and had just gratefully accepted a fourth.

'The whole thing is a miracle. All of life. From the moment I was born to this, when I mused again on the never-ending supply of beer from your magic fridge.'

Catherine sat languidly on the floor in front of a cream armchair, sipping her somethingsth gin and continuing her sentimental peanut consumption. 'That's not a miracle. Do you know how long it took to find that lamp?'

Boris scratched his head and looked thoughtful. 'Do you think if Aladdin's genie supplied beer it would be *haram*?'

'What?' Catherine looked up as she reached for a peanut.

'You know, unclean under Islamic law?'

'Didn't Aladdin precede Mohammed?'

Boris put his stubby on the table to concentrate. 'I think so, but did Aladdin ask for a fridge full of beer?'

'Not in any version I read.'

'Then perhaps that culture of abstaining from grog also preceded the Prophet.'

Catherine stretched out a leg. 'Quite possibly. Though your myopia when it comes to wishes is worrying. Perhaps Aladdin had more ambition than a never-ending six pack? You were talking about miracles? I need distractions or I'll keep thinking about a zoo-keeper.'

'It ties into your experience tonight, actually more the elephant's experience.' He absent-mindedly blessed himself. 'Life is a miracle, and the least we can do is try and minimise the damage we do to the planet and other living creatures.'

'You're going to stop being a mining magnate?'

'Exactly, or, more to the point, I'm going to stop eating meat.'

Catherine came as close to spitting gin as she ever had. 'What?'

'Vegetarian, as of tomorrow.'

'Why? Or more likely, why now?'

Boris puffed out his ample chest. 'In part, because I was talking to my mate Roger about the collective unconscious and he thought the world would be nicer if there wasn't so much death, as in animal death, because that would affect the entire make-up of the universe.'

He paused and took a long and considered sip. 'And because it's the right thing to do like a mining magnate investing all their money in unionism and renewable energy. Difference being I'm not a mining magnate, so I have to do the right thing by the miracle planet that's within my scope.'

'Couldn't you help people in a troubled country?'

'Would you come with me?'

Catherine blinked. 'I'll pay for your flights. Not much beer in Syria, though.'

'Ah, see there's the damn conundrum. I'm not giving this up,' he looked at his beer, 'and now I think of it, I would be a terrible aid worker.'

Catherine popped a peanut and shook her head as she chewed meditatively. 'I'm amazed.'

'You should, too.'

'Be amazed?'

Boris looked solemn. 'Be vegetarian.'

'Why?'

He leaned forward. 'Same reason that I should. Meat was completely necessary when we didn't have enough food, but now we live in a food surplus.' He squeezed his ample belly. 'So now we should evolve and stop killing so many things. Are you in?'

Catherine thought about it for five seconds, then chewed on a peanut. 'I was, until you made me. Now I'm going to order a hot dog and insist on my right to do so.'

Boris rolled his eyes, his hands skyward as Catherine's cat Minty jumped off him. 'Jesus, you're preaching from the right? Is this sexual frustration due to the elephant arse man?'

'Just resisting being told to do the right thing, just because you've seen the vegan light. Starts a bad precedent.'

Boris grinned. 'Shall we wait until you think it's your idea then?'

'Oh, shush.'

Hours later, sunlight danced in the steam of Catherine's milliner kettle. She blinked through it. She was a firm believer in a late night drink, if for no other reason than the lingering joy of alcohol could infuse her mornings, many of which involved speaking with very pretentious people about headwear. Sometimes this romantic idea fell flat on its over-indulged face and she spoke through a headache; but sometimes it worked. As it was, the eight o'clock news was barely over when she was called by her newest client: Philomena Kaboru. Who, after pleasantries and a brief discussion of her recent position as attaché to the Kenyan embassy in America, and subsequent Melburnian posting, began discussing her vision. 'There is no issue with price, but time is short and it is a matter of perfection, you see.'

Catherine leaned back on her chair, staring at a cobweb that she had been meaning to brush from the corner of the studio since Christmas. 'I relish a challenge.'

'I have been told that you are braver than most. The image has been with me since I was in Mississippi, years ago. As I walked down the street I passed a construction site and saw a sign with three green flags. I knew one day I would have them made into a piece of clothing.' She chuckled, the deepest chuckle Catherine had ever heard on a woman. 'It was years later I realised that this wondrous sign would become a hat, and it will be spoken of for some time, my dear.'

'I'm sure you'll look wonderful. I'll do all I can.'

As she spoke, Catherine did a computer search and found images of a strikingly beautiful black woman of about fifty years with a face that could pull off any hat.

Philomena interrupted her. 'It is not for me, Catherine, but a dear friend. I have her head measurements, and I would like this done in a week and a half for her birthday. Will that be possible?'

Catherine blinked, rearranging her week. 'Yes, I should say so, but I'll have to keep that in mind when pricing.'

'Money is not an issue,' Philomena assured her.

'Do you have a photo of the sign? I would hate for you to invest in something that simply makes you look like you're advertising a construction company.'

'I have not seen it before or since. Three flags of a strident green that came from without and within to face the sun. I shall email you my notes.'

Catherine blinked, doubling the price in her head simply for having to listen to that description. 'I should have some prototypes for you by the end of the week.'

'I appreciate that Catherine,' she said "that" with a charming "dat". Catherine could feel her hangover decreasing with each word. 'I have a good feeling about you. Make as many mistakes as you need, but make them quickly, I shall pay for your time and the materials.'

Catherine reached for her coffee, smiling imperceptibly. 'That's a good approach. I have a feeling this could take some doing.'

'It will be worth it in the name of a great gift.'

Two hours later, the steam from Catherine's kettle iron seemed to dance and wave. Philomena's demands meant that she would need a clean slate, and that meant working fast. Early autumn sunshine flowed through the large, north-facing window, making everything in the stifling room glisten. It would be hot outside later, and the people who walked past her workshop were lightly dressed. Catherine's studio was hot with a single fan blowing the steam around a room filled with hat blocks, drawers of ribbon and felts of every colour. Holly Golightly stared down at the room, cigarette holder to her mouth, a picture of ease which for once Catherine was not mirroring.

She frowned as she pressed further into the felt and the second of three blocks she was using simultaneously. The black felt, which was supposed to be taking a shape pleasing to the eye – significant in sacred geometry as part of an infinite loop but also reminiscent of 17th century French headwear – was looking to Catherine as a black waste of time and more like the *Flying Nun*'s cornette. She began working with two blocks. One for the headpiece and one for the loops.

Catherine had tried blocking linearly, but found that while the first of the three "overtures" had taken great shape, it was affected by the blocking of the remaining two. Thus, she was attempting to block each at the same time. She was using a bowler block for the outside and a dome for the middle. It could be spectacular, if it ever stopped looking so hideous. Catherine put the iron down and let her eyes rest for a second – yes, it was coming. Positive thinking was the missing ingredient and probably had been the entire time.

She squirted water from her spray bottle onto her face to cool down. In the background of her studio, the radio warbled the ten o'clock news.

'Melbourne Zoo was last night saddened by the sudden passing of elephant Dong Zei. The six-year-old female died of what is suspected to be a heart attack.' Catherine's ears pricked up as the deep voice of the male announcer was interwoven with Georgia Potter's.

'It's a terrible loss,' Georgia said, adding, 'even though Dong Zei had been ill recently it's a dreadful time of sadness for our zoo family.'

As the announcer moved to the next story, Catherine got an itch at the back of her neck. Beau hadn't mentioned any sickness; in fact, he had been clear that Dong Zei was in perfect health.

For the next hour, she moulded the felt and by the end had something suitably garish. A few hours of pouncing and sewing and this could be a masterpiece. It would certainly stand out on her website.

It was two o'clock and the slate was clearer for Philomena's hat. Catherine gave herself the rest of the day off. The beer garden was calling her and she would yield to that wild siren. Or would have, had her phone not rung at that very moment.

'This is Catherine.'

A deep voice. 'Hi. Me.'

'The astounding Mr Hacska.'

'How'd you find that out?'

'Believe it or not, the moment I mentioned a zoologist named Beau several of my colleagues knew who you were.'

He cleared his throat. 'And where I've been.'

'Naughty man, I didn't mention that.' Her eyes moved to the horizon as she heard him snort.

'Are you always this forward?'

She gripped her balcony happily, liking that he got it. 'Women have been polite and therefore oppressed for centuries. I'm not even scratching the surface of equilibrium.'

'This is exactly the conversation I needed, thanks for not disappointing.'

'I generally only disappoint people I'm related to. How's the post-mortem?'

'Feels more like a witch hunt right now. Anyway, not why I was calling.'

Catherine leaned forward, the wind cooling her skin after the humidity of the studio. 'Stick to your guns. Tell me about it later.'

'So, I can cook you dinner?'

'No, but you can buy me dinner. Glasgow Palace, Brunswick, whenever you finish. I'm going there now.'

'Does that mean you'll be drunk?'

'I don't get drunk. The world just gets more interesting.' He was chuckling as she hung up.

Two minutes later the phone rang again, private number. Catherine answered, 'Continued calling won't keep me sober. It's early days fella, know your place.'

There was a silence on the line. Catherine's face fell as coldness swept through her.

'I was ringing for an update on progress,' said a clipped voice with an African accent. 'This is Catherine, correct?'

A hand went to Catherine's purple "Ispoti" hat, which she had chosen for the afternoon. 'Philomena, what a lovely surprise.'

A sigh came across the line. 'Ah good, I don't have the wrong number. How is progress?'

Catherine eyed her clock. She had last spoken to this woman, for the first time six hours ago. 'I've had a look at your notes, but I've other hats to work on.'

'Ah.' There was a pause. 'I understand. You will start it tomorrow?'

Catherine looked at the orange hat and calculated her time, giving an hour for sleep. 'Yes, that should be in order.'

'Oh good. If you've seen my notes you will have seen who it's for, a special lady.'

Catherine smiled, turning to her laptop. 'I'll be on it tomorrow, if not tonight.' She crossed her fingers as they sailed across her touchpad, reopening the email.

'Excellent Catherine, I shall not call again tonight.'

'Thank you,' Catherine hoped she sounded firm.

As she hung up she went through the email again. Yes, the notes were in order: three sails, striking jade green, measurements. Then there was a photo file she hadn't opened. She double clicked and...

Grace Chichester smiled back at her. Wearing a terrible fascinator at a racecourse.

Goose bumps rose up Catherine's arms and neck simultaneously. She was making a hat for Grace Chichester. Minister of the State Parliament. Champion of the ugly side of conservative politics and a tormentor of young milliners in their school days.

Catherine's face fell. Her mind went blank for a few seconds, before thoughts came in a frenzy. If Grace knew who made it she would be awful. If, by chance, she liked it then Catherine would have contributed to Grace's happiness, which was also awful. Catherine couldn't win.

It was intolerable.

Perhaps it was a set-up? Grace would do that. Catherine could imagine her organising behind the façade of parliamentary privilege.

She lay on the couch and Minty immediately came and lay on top of her. For the next twenty minutes Catherine stroked her cat and thought about rivals, conspiracies, hats and dying elephants. The fact that Grace would be so pleased by her getting this worked up didn't improve the situation.

After a time, she remembered that there were one billion light years of empty space in the universe, completely devoid of all matter or dark matter. She remembered that no one knew why. The best minds in the business surmised it had something to do with dark energy. Catherine had only met three people, ever, who knew the difference between dark matter and dark energy. Boris had assumed she was talking about *The Dark Crystal*. It cheered her up immensely. It always did.

Boris had a gin for her on the bar as she walked in. She took up her usual position on the north side of the bar, with a view of the front bar tables, stage, the back room, the walkway from the beer garden and most regularly, Boris.

'You looked a little serious today, hard day at the office?'

'T'was middling. I would love to have conquered, instead I merely toiled.'

'And so say three-quarters of the global artisans at this happy hour of five.' His eyes moved to the clock. 'Three o'clock.'

Catherine toasted his ability to tell the time and sage context regarding the difficulty of art, hats and poetry all at once.

'Then I got a call from a new and demanding client, who wants me to do a very tricky job as a present for–' she gave a drumroll on the bar, '–Grace Chichester.'

He threw a tea towel over his shoulder. 'I shall make the next one a double.'

'I like the thought, but hold off, I have a date tonight.'

'The elephant man?'

Catherine checked her nails over her glass. As usual, a disaster. 'I assure you he is not hideous at all.'

'Not that you're shallow.'

'Hmm.'

Boris was called to serve another customer, leaving Catherine thinking about hats and whether arsenic could be sewn into them without ruining the aesthetic. It was discombobulating wanting to do a good job for someone you loathed.

Boris walked past. 'You'll be fine. She's a lot like you.'

Catherine's eyes hardened. 'That's a dreadful thing to say.'

'She's strong-willed, intelligent and more than a bit stubborn.'

Catherine's palm was on the bar. 'You saw her on television and hated her immediately.'

'I hated her politics. Her manner reminded me of someone I quite like. Besides, you're a milliner, did you think all your clients would be socialists?'

Catherine pointed at him with her glass. 'You're on thin ice.'

'Only because I'm right. Another?' Boris took the gin down from the shelf.

'And just when I was wondering why I kept you around.'

Boris wiped his hands in a tea towel. 'I heard about the elephant. They were saying it had been sick for a while.'

'Yes.' Catherine looked along the bar to see the light play on the varnished tables. 'Though that contradicts my zoo-keeper man friend. So I'm open to that being a pile of dung.'

'A mystery for you?'

'Oh, surely zoology is beyond me. I'm more focused on sabotaging hats and being swept off my feet this evening.'

Boris gestured towards the bar snacks. 'You'll need some sustenance. Peanuts?'

'I'll be quite happy with this.' She raised her glass. 'How goes the herbivorism?'

He looked up, smiling happily. 'Honestly?'

'Of course.'

'I'm aware I could be riding a wave of smug.'

Catherine laughed, 'My dear, if the world was as self-aware as you there would be less splits in the left wing of politics.'

Boris shrugged modestly. 'I see my role as a unifier, with spinach.'

Hours later, there was chatter in her ears and the wounds of the day had long been washed away by the heal-all that was the beer garden at the Glasgow Palace. In the gentle autumn sunshine, sparrows fluttered between tables and over the umbrellas, chasing vinegar flies, mosquitoes and discarded chips.

After a session of genial conversation with the usual suspects of failed academics, rock stars and criminals who counted as her closest drinking buddies, Catherine was joined by the handsome Beau Hacska. He looked wearily resplendent in his khaki zoo-keeper's uniform. He kissed her easily and showed no signs of worry about the conventions for a first date. He also hadn't been worried about how many gin and tonics had passed her lips, and although he turned out to be vegetarian was completely tolerant of omnivores.

'You should tell Boris, could be a free pint in it for you.'

Beau looked at his half-finished drink. 'Could be worth all the steak I've missed, thanks.'

'Tell me what they're saying about the elephant?'

His face darkened. 'They're saying two things which annoy me. They're saying Dong Zei may have been sick for some time.'

He sipped his drink.

'And?'

'They're implying I was negligent in my care of her.'

'Oh.'

He pursed his lips. 'They're being very nice about it, but it's not pleasant.'

'Are they wrong?'

He put a hand through his dark hair, and scratched the back of his head.

'I like that you ask, rather than just be on my side because I'm here.' He leant forward. 'On point one, I don't think so. I've worked with those elephants for eight months now, I have seen two of them get sick and recover.'

Catherine watched the way the light behind him played in his hair. He had a nice voice. 'So, that renders the second point moot.'

He finished his drink. 'You'd think so. Don't worry, they're being gentle about it. Ian Bradbury practically embraced me after he had finished his meeting with Georgia. It's all pending investigation.'

'Do you get to be part of that investigation?'

'Bloody hope so.' He stood up to go to the bar. He didn't ask if she wanted another. Just took her empty glass.

They passed the rest of the meal entirely focused on the pitfalls of Australian politics and the gradual constipated groan of the global variety shifting to the right end of the spectrum. Catherine had a terrifying moment worrying that he was perfect and was almost relieved to see him bring out a tobacco pouch.

She watched Beau light up a post-meal cigarette with fleeting jealousy. It didn't compute with her identity that other people should enjoy life more than her, even Beau. He had a cowlick of hair that looked all the better for not being deliberate or ironic. He was one of the few who could pull off a moustache. The fact that he chose not to made him a gentleman.

'Do you really enjoy those?'

He looked at the cigarette. 'Do they bother you?'

She shook her head, coming forward into the smoke. 'Only that I've never understood the attraction.'

He smiled. 'If you haven't worked it out, then it's not for you. Consider it a blessing.'

Having sniffed the air, she leaned back in her seat, satisfied. 'I do. I like the idea but they taste like burning wood being sucked into my lungs.'

'Mine too,' he said, inhaling deeply. 'Amazing what you can get used to when you start a habit at fifteen.'

'Should have done yoga.'

'These were easier to find than my chakras.'

At some point in the evening Catherine had rested her feet on his lap. She rearranged herself to increase blood flow to her right leg.

'So aside from being embraced by Ian and everyone staring at you like you missed something, how was work?'

'Pretty sad. The director sent out an email regarding the autopsy.'

'Could you do it?'

'I'm qualified, but I'd have to plead my case against conflict of interest. There's another on staff who might do it.'

'You know him?'

'We've spoken; he's been Bradbury's protégé for years. I've only known him since I came back from Europe. He's quiet.'

'And?'

'There's not much to him. Being a keeper is a trade, some do it because they love animals, some because they suck with people.'

'Whereas you're a monkey-loving softie.'

He stubbed out his cigarette. 'Hence the vegetarianism.'

She smiled. 'Not vegan, though.'

'I don't believe in a higher power, but I'm close when I eat good cheese.'

Catherine laughed and watched him smile, enjoying it. 'I heard Georgia Potter on the radio today pushing the sick elephant idea.'

Beau looked at his cigarette and shook his head slowly. 'I really do think it's bullshit, even if she does say it on the radio.'

'I thought so.'

They sat in silence a while, watching an animated game of table tennis occurring a few metres away. The night was warm, the pub full of uni students and people who looked like they were in bands lazing around. Boris wandered through the crowd collecting glasses and smiled discreetly at Catherine, the way he usually did when she was on a date.

'Why would Georgia say Dong Zei was sick?'

Beau took a pull of his beer. 'I'm not sure, and it could only be my ego saying that she wasn't. I just get the feeling that there's more to this. As for Georgia, I can't work her out. She's only been on the board a couple of years. Near as I can tell it's a prestige thing rather than any love of the zoo or the animals. That said, Ian Bradbury thinks she's brilliant. She's what brought him to the zoo.'

He scratched his chin. 'I've been with Dong Zei every day for the past six weeks and there was no warning.'

'Did anyone comment on it at work in your favour?'

He smiled again. 'No, aside from a hug from Bradbury it was all daggers and avoidance.'

'So, none of the other keepers are on your team?'

'I'm new, I got the job over a lot of other qualified people and if Bradbury thinks I might have missed something there's a lot of people who will follow his lead.'

'Isn't he?'

'What? A wanker? Yes, but he knows his stuff, too.'

Catherine's gin was evaporating. She found Boris' eyes as he was clearing plates and gave a nod.

'I guess it's a bad look when an animal dies unexpectedly.' Beau grinned without humour. 'Personally, I think it's worse when you're lying to the public and your staff.'

'And finding a fall guy.'

For a second Beau looked about a hundred. She took his wrist, noticing a scar across it. 'You don't have to fall.'

'Sorry,' He smiled, unconvincingly. 'I assure you I have no intention.'

Catherine got up, nodding at Beau's almost empty pint. His smile became more genuine.

The drinks were on the bar when Catherine arrived. Boris nodded mid-pour. 'Looks good.'

'Looks great,' said Catherine, picking up the drinks.

'Be careful though, I hear he's an arse man.'

'Up yours too, Shakhovskoy,' Catherine called cheerily.

Beau was smoking and watching the ping pong when she returned. He took the pint gratefully. 'Thanks.'

Catherine raised her gin. 'To Dong Zei.'

'I'm told you're a kind of investigator,' he leaned closer.

Catherine was glad they were both watching the ping pong and she didn't have to look at his face.

'I know a lot less than you, Ian or even Georgia about animals.'

'One of the blokes in there was telling me you're good at reading people.'

Catherine had hoped this would be strictly pleasure. 'Some better than others. Are you asking for help?'

'Not really, I could just use a smart friend in the next few days.'

He was smiling at something going on in the game. He had a lovely look when he was happy. Catherine thought that was worth preserving.

'I can be a pair of eyes on your shoulder. You tell me what they do, I'll read them.'

He turned to her, smiling his lopsided smile. 'What do you want in return?'

She kissed him lightly. He tasted of smoke and life. 'Warmth.'

3

My ego survives on the smell of an oily rag.
~ Boris Shakhovskoy

Boris felt a rising panic. He stared at it in his hands, pink and lifeless, as it dripped onto the laminex floor. The blood drained from his face. His eyes closed and his tongue ran over lips that had gone dry, seeing a future forever altered.

This was all because he was trying to do the right thing. He had been so careful, he had loved, but not too much. Now it was finished and it all went so wrong. Catherine could never help him. In one mistake, it was over.

His favourite t-shirt – the Mr Spock, with Leonard Nimoy staring impassively out to the middle distance – had run pink. Boris bit his lip, breathed deeply and tried to think of what Mr Spock would do. Around him dryers and washers droned in his ears. He looked to the clock at the end of the room as if to get a time of death. It was 11.44am.

'Oh Christ, what did you do?'

He looked up and saw a young woman, her blue eyes wide with a horror he was feeling, her right hand pushing a handful of dark hair back to inspect the awful damage as her left hand hauled a basket of washing nearly as big as she was.

'I broke something special.' He looked from the t-shirt in his hands to her. She hoisted her basket upright and placed a hand on his shoulder.

'Wow, that is vintage too.' Her hand ran from his shoulder down his back. 'Don't worry, you can still buy those.'

She turned and began feeding her washing to the adjacent machine.

Boris stood slowly, all the while looking at the t-shirt. He breathed deeply and then slapped it into his basket of wet clothes.

'What did the damage?' She looked over her shoulder as she spoke, her hand still moving to load the machine. She had a full face with a ring through the left side of her nose. Her tired eyes were no longer concerned, but still showed sympathy. She wore dark jeans and a loose t-shirt, ripped by design in a way that many just couldn't pull off. She managed it possibly because of her short stature. Underneath, a plain white undergarment covered her chest. Boris hated that he noticed that.

'My new towels,' he said ruefully, pulling them out of the washer. They were still a striking red, but had been more brilliant forty-five minutes prior. 'New friggin' towels. I don't know what I was thinking.'

'Ahh, you were just doing the washing. There's honour there.'

He picked up his basket. 'I'll get over it.'

'Start a new trend, wear it pink.'

Boris smiled at the thought, 'I don't think so.'

'Pink is for girls?' She looked at him carnivorously.

'No, no, it's not that. I just loved that t-shirt.'

'Have you considered, sir,' her voice modulated in a way that made Boris stare at her, 'that your aversion to wearing the shirt pink is motivated by an illogical idea of masculinity.'

She poured detergent into the machine and kicked the front loader closed. Boris couldn't help but smile.

'That's a pretty good Spock.'

She didn't smile but moved her head sharply, as if to hear better. 'Further, I would point out that your emotional response is also illogical and in no way productive.'

Boris stood up, summoning his best Bones McCoy: 'Dammit Spock something awful has happened, even your Vulcan heart should see that.'

She grinned and held out a hand. 'Nice. I'm Molly.'

'Boris. You've brightened a dark moment in my life.'

'You'll be all right, put it in the dryer and see.' She gestured to the rack of dryers on the far wall, smiling. 'Cheer up, Charlie.'

'I'm just around the corner, I'll use my washing line.'

'All right. See you round.'

It was only when he was outside and halfway towards his flat that he realised that using the dryer would have meant a continued conversation.

With a girl. Who did a good Spock impersonation and liked his t-shirt, and thought doing the washing was noble. He thought about going back and stating that his washing line had broken down. Tried the words out. Shook his head and kept walking.

Through layers of sleep, Catherine knew he had gone early. Kissed her cheek, was quiet. She liked that. She woke again hours later to the smells of skin in her room. She was about to open the window when she decided to let it linger in the air, mixing with the coffee she made. In what was becoming a terrible habit, she checked her emails before showering, only to find an urgent order for three blue pillbox hats. Her phone vibrated. A text from Philomena: *Good morning Catherine. I hope you are prepared for a productive day.* Catherine blinked at it then recalled she'd made hats for irritating people before and that only made the gin their money bought tastier.

At her work bench she listened to a podcast on vegetarianism, keen for an edge over Boris' argument. The speaker verged on preachy, but then backed it up with facts. Humans had eaten meat since about five million years ago, this did not necessarily coincide with our taking over the planet but there was a semi-plausible link to be made. As the podcast finished, the question on Catherine's mind was: well, we're in charge now, so why not stop killing animals and enjoy some awesome falafel?

She didn't feel like falafel. In fact, the idea made her not want falafel for a while. What was irritating about the whole thing was the knowledge that in two months' time Boris would be back to his love of all things chicken and crumbed. Still, it distracted her from thinking about Beau, Grace, torture or anything else she should not be indulging in.

With the pillboxes on the way she moved to begin Philomena's hat and pulled the drawer open for the green felt. Only to find a moth lying dead next to a mothball. While it was gratifying to know that the mothballs were doing their job, it would have been better if she had been doing hers, and had stayed on top of the ordering. This would mean either a three-day wait for green felt if she went through the normal ordering – which due to Philomena's timeframe would be unacceptable – or a trip into Sanderson's in town to stock up. Her thoughts turned briefly to Philomena's now prophetic text.

'Yes, yes,' Catherine muttered to herself and remembered that three days ago she had said that she would do the ordering and then go to the pub, but Boris had called and she had gone to the pub. Perfect. This was Boris' fault. She headed downstairs to the Vespa.

'No, no,' was her response four minutes later, when she remembered coming into the small garage just as her Vespa ran out of petrol after a late night kebab run. Worse, it was a night Boris wasn't there, so it was going to be difficult to blame him. Regardless, the Vespa was now unusable and she would either need to take a jerry can to the petrol station on Dawson Street or take a train.

She heard a train hoot north on the Upfield line and began running before she was even aware of the decision. Soon she was panting and not enjoying the stitch that came far too quickly. Even walking she made the train easily.

After some thirty minutes of commuting, purchasing and meditating on making mature choices – and how this was Boris' fault – Catherine had three rolls of green felt under her arm and a spring in her step. Anytime she despaired of the hat-making world or the people she had to create hats for, the tonic was to spend time in the supply shops. Feeling that amazing potential that comes from row upon row of dazzling blank canvasses waiting to be turned into something beautiful. While she had paid more for buying in retail, her soul felt better for it, and when she got on the 1.55 to Upfield she was content.

Then she remembered that this was all for Grace and she scowled, sitting and exhaling loudly at a window seat.

A leg brushed hers and she moved to allow a man to sit opposite her. He was tall with brown hair brushed back behind his ears to fall just short of his bearded jawline. He wore a red-checked shirt and blue jeans, his body language exuded confidence without seeming to be a leer. Catherine was about to ask if they had met when he grinned and started whistling.

He whistled like a drunken gondolier and took his sunglasses off slowly, almost tenderly. He had ditched *Total Eclipse of the Heart* for Tom Jones' *What's New, Pussycat?* Catherine suspected he may be Welsh or at least had a predilection for Welsh singers – hardly a hanging offence.

She didn't join in this time, but simply watched until he finished the first verse with a particularly impressive octaval flourish and then bowed his head theatrically. His hair flopped almost to his knee as she applauded. Behind him, other commuters relaxed, relieved that a fight was not about to break out. He brought his head up and his fringe fell impossibly back into place as if it were not so much hair as a very obedient pet.

He presented his hand. 'Andy.' His accent came from posh Edinburgh, or possibly Fife, which explained his lack of tan after an Australia summer.

She shook his hand briefly. 'Catherine. I'm not sure we should ever speak, Andy.'

He nodded, understanding. 'It's tempting, isn't it? I'm not sure about you, but I'm only going to be a disappointment from here.'

Catherine leaned back in her seat, giving him an appraising look. 'I agree. Unless you're a charismatic acrobat with your own jet and thrilling set of travel anecdotes, you're doomed.'

He smiled grimly and looked down at his hands. 'I'm in admin.'

'It's a lost cause I'm afraid.'

He looked back up. 'I've been to Beijing?'

'That would have been impressive one hundred years ago,' Catherine sighed, as if resigned.

'Cairo?'

She brought out her phone and began checking it. 'Two hundred,' she said dismissively.

'I've been to paradise, but never seen Priscilla?'

She looked at him sharply, and put her phone away. 'That's brought you one life, but you're still on the precipice.'

He stopped to think during the train announcement that they were coming to Macaulay Station. 'I'd really like to spend more time in Geelong.'

'That's just conversational suicide.'

'I was uncomfortable with you holding all the cards, you know I can whistle but you're an enigma wrapped in a secret...'

'Wrapped in a stylish green cardigan. Very well. I will tell you that I'm great at cricket.'

He leaned in, brows dancing. 'Why would you tell a Scotsman that?'

'I'm mirroring your conversational suicide.'

'Very clever. Would you like to come to Geelong with me?'

'Not tonight dear, I have a headache.'

'So does Geelong.'

'It's a city. Do you mean all the people?'

'All the people, every single one. Reaching for the Panadol and wishing they knew more about Chinese medicine. Complaining to their partners, losing patience with their children. What's worse, they don't even know why. They haven't a clue.'

He spoke a lot with his hands – they came together and then both sets of fingers gestured gently towards himself. 'But I know. They all have a headache because you're not there.'

Catherine leaned in as the train turned towards Royal Park. 'I feel for them. It must be hard, but the sacrifice is too great. I shall not go south with you.'

'Is it Geelong or is it me? You can tell me, I can take it.' Andy breathed in, puffing out his chest.

Catherine waited a full ten seconds, never breaking eye contact, even though she knew that if she turned her eyes a little to the left she would see the zoo receding in the distance. 'It's Geelong, Andy.'

He brought up his hands in triumph. Then he looked concerned. 'That's wonderful, but I see why people say Melburnians are elitist.'

'I might like Geelong. How do you know I wasn't being polite to you?'

'Because a gypsy woman told me that anyone I whistle with will find me irresistible.'

He brought his mouth together in a pucker that was part pre-whistle and part suggestion.

Catherine looked out the window. 'I don't believe in prophecy.'

'But I believe in whistling.'

'And you continue to do so. The world needs true believers.'

'You don't believe in whistling?'

'Believe it? I've seen it.'

He smiled and stopped for a minute. After their rapid fire conversation Catherine was grateful for a moment to think. For some reason, she thought of an elephant.

'Perhaps Geelong was too ambitious. How about a drink?' he suggested.

'Certainly sometime, but your timing's off.'

He cocked his head. 'Married?'

'Not even engaged, but your timing's off.'

'How about I look out for you on a train?'

'That's a very good idea.'

He gestured out the window with his eyes, 'It's your stop.'

Indeed, the train was approaching Anstey Station. She picked up her felt and stood as Andy shifted his long legs to facilitate her ease of passage.

Catherine rewarded him with a wink. 'See you round, whistler.'

'Aye, hope my timing improves.'

'Never know your luck.'

The doors closed and Catherine walked into the afternoon sun. She was surprised at herself. A handsome man had asked to buy her a drink and she had said no.

Years ago, she had worked out there was a collective unconsciousness with men. They seemed to arrive in waves, banded together in a bid to confuse and flatter her.

As she unlocked the door of her apartment and put the rolls of felt down, the amount of work between her and recreation seemed enormous. The amount of work needed on Philomena Keburo's three green flags of fashion triumph, plus the fortitude not to spin out about it being for Grace was considerable. As ever, she was considering how convenient cloning will be, and how human endeavour mixed with our narcissism make this inevitable.

Perhaps that's why she shivered as she answered the ringing phone. Or perhaps it was something else.

'This is Catherine.'

'Catherine.' Boris sounded like he was being held over a fire.

'Boris?'

'Have you seen the news in the past half hour?'

'No.'

'A keeper has been mauled at the zoo; he's in intensive care. They haven't released his name, but he's thirty-two. I think it could be Beau.'

4

Don't tell me animals are boring, not one animal has ever tried to sell me something.

~ Beau Hacska

The taxi driver's name was Roger; he was in his sixties. He had a ruddy face, a discolouration on his left hand where a wedding band had once been, and when he saw Catherine's face he turned the radio off. Roger was all right.

As they sped down Royal Parade Catherine worked hard to keep her tone even. After listening to hold music and then pressing through three menu choices, she was talking to a human being at the zoo.

'I've told you I have no information to give regarding the keeper's identity or his condition, I'm sorry–'

Catherine slapped the taxi window. 'And I'm telling you that I'm not from *The Sun*, Channel Nine or news.com. I just want a yes or no answer. Is the keeper who was hurt Beau Hacska?'

'Please hold.'

Catherine leaned her head against the glass, watching the university go by slowly as they inched towards yet another red light. She thought of hanging up and trying Beau's number again. It had rung out twice. But Catherine knew that if someone else had been badly hurt at the zoo, Beau wouldn't be answering his phone anyway.

The hold music was terrible, worse for being interposed with a nasal voice advising she could buy zoo memberships online.

Catherine leaned forward in her seat to relieve the pain in her stomach and she had to focus to breathe. The chatty part of her brain reminded her that she had known him less than forty-eight hours. Her gut instinct fought back, because you don't need to know someone long to not want them dismembered.

She caught Roger's eye in the rear-view mirror. He had puffy half-moons of skin under each eye, making Catherine think of a mournful St Bernard dog. He smiled wanly. 'They won't tell you, luv.'

The music stopped. 'Hello, thanks for holding. I'm unable to tell you anything about the identity of the keeper hurt. There will be a statement made in due course. I'm so sorry.' The voice, of a younger man by the sound of it, seemed to mean these words.

Catherine's reply was cold. 'One day, you'll be in a car racing to a hospital and the situation will be made worse by an idiot who's obeying the rules. Consider it your punishment for not thinking when you could have made a difference in another human's life. We've had four billion years of evolution so you could play it safe. What a joke.'

She ended the call to the sound of him spluttering. Roger gave her a bigger smile. 'Nobody tells anyone nothin' these days.'

They arrived at the hospital. Roger killed the engine as she got her purse out, her hands shaking.

'No charge luv, hope he's orright.'

Catherine smiled at him, too stunned for words. She ran from the cab up the stairs of the hospital. Hoping that any second Beau would come out and laugh at her for getting so worked up. He didn't, and the glass doors moved to let her in.

The receptionist looked up as Catherine came toward her and had 'What name please?' out before Catherine had finished running.

'Beau Hacska.'

She nodded. Typed. 'Spelling?' she asked, without looking up.

Catherine guessed.

'There's nothing coming up.'

Catherine grinned like a loon. 'Maybe try with a 'c', he would have come in an ambulance.'

There was a gap of a few seconds, where Catherine's guts began to untwist.

The receptionist looked up again. 'I found him. He's here.'

Catherine made an unladylike sound and she crumpled, her hand gripping the reception counter.

'Are you all right?'

Catherine pushed herself upright. 'I barely know him.'

The girl looked puzzled, Catherine shook her head. 'Where is he?'

'He's in surgery, you can wait on the first floor.'

'Thanks.'

'Are you sure you're okay?'

Catherine walked on.

She felt the punch drunk quiet that comes with any break to unthinking invincibility, but it was subdued. She knew she couldn't make the surgeons work harder, or stop the blood from doing what blood did. Catherine walked through well-lit halls and heard the hum of lifts. She quietly said his name under her breath, along with the names of twenty different deities. She didn't believe they were listening, but on days like this, you don't mind the possibility of being wrong.

The waiting room was empty. A blue line ran along the floor leading to the surgical theatre. Catherine sat on a pale vinyl chair, still chanting under her breath and grateful that there was no television. In Catherine's limited experience, all television got forty per cent worse when you were stuck inside a hospital.

She checked her phone, Boris had texted offering his support. She didn't text back but checked a news site which had a brief report that a male keeper, thirty-two years old, was in hospital after being mauled by African wild dogs. More to come.

African wild dogs. Catherine searched for an image and shivered. They were big eared and mottled dogs, slightly smaller than an Alsatian, minus any sign of domestication. She wondered how many there were. Had it been more than two, she doubted he had a chance.

She could feel a sob forming when the far door opened. A woman in her forties powered towards her with a purposeful stride and glasses almost steaming.

Georgia Potter moved past her and peered into the opaque glass windows of the surgical theatre. After a full minute she turned.

'Which one are you with?'

Catherine raised an eyebrow. 'I don't follow.'

Georgia was gripping her handbag so tightly it looked like it would break in two. 'Which paper? You don't have a camera so you can't be with a TV station. Who pays your wages?' Her voice was part bravado, part vibrato.

'Cougars.'

Georgia blinked, Catherine continued. 'Mostly cougars. Though some men in their fifties who are trying to channel the bard by hiding a bald spot. Then there's bright young things looking fabulous at the races, many a bridesmaid has worn my headwear and let's not forget, because I live in Brunswick, there's trustafarian uni students wearing glamourous headwear ironically.'

Catherine stood and walked slowly towards the clearly abashed Georgia, holding out her hand. 'Catherine Kint, milliner, we've met twice.'

Georgia swallowed. 'I introduced you to Ian Bradbury, you were wearing tan boots and a pillbox hat. Someone told me later that they'd seen you kissing…'

She turned and glanced at the surgical theatre.

'I'm so sorry Catherine,' Georgia said, and hugged her close.

Catherine's control wavered, as it often did in stressful times when someone started being nice to her. For a moment, they were just two women, who barely knew each other, experiencing a tragedy.

Georgia broke the embrace and stood back, picking up her handbag, which she'd dropped.

'How did you find out?'

'The news, a friend called me; we knew Beau's age. How bad is it?'

Georgia turned away from Catherine and put a shaking hand to her temple.

'I wasn't there, though I saw the ground afterwards. It's not good, I'm afraid.'

'Has this happened before?'

'Not in Melbourne. Nothing like this has happened for as long as I can remember. Occasionally keepers get hurt, that's why I thought you were a journo. They'll be arriving soon. We live and breathe safety at the zoo.' She closed her eyes. 'Not a good choice of phrase.'

'I'm not a journo. Relax.'

'God, the idea of Beau. The people who will be watching us. This is…' She trailed off and sat down. Minutes passed after this, the two women silent. They both periodically looked towards the opaque glass of the theatre.

A door opened, with more staff from the zoo trickling in. Then came cameras and journalists. Everyone shared the lack of news. That it could be hours. Catherine found out there had been more than four dogs involved. Her stomach flipped and she moved over to a window and watched the first sprays of a rain shower tap against it.

While he chewed, he looked out the across the lively room to the pub windows. Outside the world was still moving, it was even raining a little. The planet hadn't stopped turning because he was eating a salad. He hadn't become any noticeably wiser. His hand gripped his belly, still soft , still generous, still there. It occurred to him that eating anything wasn't going to change it, and that if he just learned to love this moment he would have that body he had lost somewhere between starting and finishing university.

'It's an exercise in loving the moment,' he said to no one.

He looked at it again. Salad. On his plate, taking up the entirety of his evening meal. When he could be having a parmigiana. It was a hard thing to reconcile. Likewise, his drink was soda water when he could have coke or red lemonade, or squash. He took a sip. It was like nothing, with bubbles, which somehow made it worse.

'No, I love it.' It was Taoism, he decided, finding the vinegar sweet. He kept chewing. Even bloody vinegar would taste like something. He crunched a mouthful of lettuce and radish and wondered if chips would help. Salad and chips, it could be the next big culinary thing. Perhaps that was where he would make his mark on the world.

'You're not wearing it.' A voice came from behind him; he turned around and saw the beautiful short girl from the laundromat. He giggled, and a small piece of lettuce fell from his beard to the floor between them.

'It wasn't dry.'

'Ah, the old washing line doesn't come through.'

He gestured outside. 'Not when it rains.'

She looked past him to the windows. 'Bummer. But you didn't hurt the earth though, did you? Dryers are bad.'

Boris nodded, running his tongue over his teeth surreptitiously. 'They do dry clothes very well though.'

'Yep.' She was drinking a Coopers beer. Boris wondered how the hell he hadn't noticed her walking in.

'Hey, you're on salad. Diet or vego?'

'Vego.' It was the first time he had said the word to a stranger. It felt odd.

She smiled. 'Yeah, me too.'

'I haven't seen you in here before, are you a local?'

'I've just moved from Gosford.' She looked outside. 'I came down to study.'

'Welcome.'

'Are you the manager?'

'No.'

She ran a hand through her thick dark hair. 'You seem like a manager.'

'Really?' He puffed up a little.

'Well, you're older than all the other staff.'

He breathed out, huffily. 'Thanks.'

'I'll leave you to your salad.'

'You don't have to.' Boris realised how stupid this sounded while in mid-sentence, but it was too late.

She looked at him with a quiet smile. 'I'll come find you later when I need a refill.'

He watched her violet leggings and denim skirt as she sashayed away. Boris looked at his salad. He hated the world.

He played it cool when she came for a refill.

The third time, she asked about his favourite vego restaurants, of which he had none. Then Leon, the real manager, called him away to change a keg. When he returned, the chat continued, even after Boris had knocked off. They were talking tofu.

'No, it's really the most wonderful thing, it can absorb any flavour on earth.' She had moved onto wine. Boris had his knockoff pint. The beer garden was almost deserted.

'Then why does it taste like nothing, or at least nothing nice?'

'Well, you can take that a couple of ways. Either it's actually from space which is mostly nothing nice, or it's a reflection of life and it's what you make of it.'

Inside his head, Boris swooned. She spoke the way he thought when he was very, very tired. Still, he was keen to improve his new life and tofu tasting good would do that. Outwardly, he kept playing it cool.

'Neither of those are appealing.'

He took a meditative sip to show he was serious.

'Or you just haven't had it cooked very well.'

'Right. You may have me there.'

A silence hung. This was the moment where he should say something debonair about taking her to Lentil as Anything or something. Yet he stalled. He stalled because he had enjoyed the last fifteen minutes so much that he didn't want to ruin it. So, he just took a long drink of his beer and wondered if something clever would come out of his mouth when he finished.

She watched him, then looked over his shoulder and said, 'Tell you what, you take me to dinner and I'll order for you.'

Forty-five seconds later, when he had stopped choking, it was agreed upon for the following Thursday. Boris celebrated by making wheezing sounds.

Molly grabbed his shoulder, her face concerned. 'Are you all right?'

'Yes.' Boris wiped his eyes again.

Her hand moved up to his right cheek. 'The restaurant will blow your mind. Chefs have to be better when there's no easy meat option.'

'I've never been to a steakless restaurant.'

'Ever had soy milk?'

'No.'

'Try it tomorrow, with something you would usually have with cow's milk and call me.'

'Why?'

'I'm going to school you in one of life's true lessons.'

At ten, a doctor came and made a brief statement. Mr Hacska had survived the surgery and was now in an induced coma. It was unknown how long he would be in this state but almost certainly for the next twenty-four hours. There was no point in staying. A journalist asked about brain damage, there was no comment. The doctor asked if there were any family or partners in the group waiting. Catherine felt Georgia's eyes on her but she didn't move.

Outside, Catherine walked slowly past the orange bricks of the hospital, seeing every one and imagining the hands that put them in place decades before. She saw the streetlamps and felt the concrete under her feet, all made by hands that had had their time and then left the work, left the place or left the planet. Everything moved forwards, a procession that we all experience for what seems like a moment, and a lifetime in that moment.

Catherine walked towards Nicholson Street. The rain had cleared and now stars sparkled dimly against the city lights. She turned as a tram rattled to the nearby stop, before realising it wasn't her line. She stood in the cool night, watching the faces on the tram and imagining the lives that lay within. All of them thinking of futures or pasts when all that would come would be distractions and then, a silence.

She knew this feeling would pass; this quiet sad certainty would go. Death, or almost death, was the only thing that could quiet most people's minds. Catherine sometimes wondered if everyone enjoyed it as much as her. She supposed they did. There are very few times in anyone's life where you can think in a straight line.

The Exhibition building was lit up and she wondered who the architect was. Who had made this their great work, and why did it matter? Stain the ground enough and they will remember your name. She didn't know the architect's name; the architect wouldn't know Beau Hacska's name; or how his hands felt when his shirt was off. Even Tutankhamun, who was covered in gold and held a dagger that was wrought from a meteor, would fade. Yes, she knew his name, three thousand years later, but he'd died at seventeen, so what bloody good did it do him?

These thoughts took her to Royal Parade, where a tram's yellow lights blinked at her in the middle distance. The number nineteen would take her home.

Boris stayed after she left. Molly hadn't wanted him to walk her home, and he only asked twice. Afterwards he fell into a conversation about football and whether the distraction from the global crisis of population and warmth was a tribute to humanity's love of problems that it could solve by beating someone rather than listening to someone.

He had been thinking about Molly and wistfully looking out the glass door when he saw Catherine.

One look at her and he remembered: Beau. He stood, wavering only a little, and unlocked the door. 'It was him?'

Catherine nodded.

Boris felt a kick in the guts. 'Oh no.'

She fell into him for an embrace that lasted a long time. The glass door closed quietly behind her.

Catherine broke away. 'He's still alive, in a coma.'

'Why didn't you ring me?'

'I did.'

Boris reached into his back pocket and pulled his phone out. 'On silent. Catherine, I'm sorry.'

'It's all right.' She surveyed the chairs on the tables and noted Boris' nearly finished pot. 'Fancy a drink at mine?'

'For sure.'

5

There's cruelty everywhere, that doesn't mean I have to like it.
~ Boris Shakhovskoy

Catherine woke with the dim light of dawn creeping up the wall and remembered everything. Sometimes, after a trauma, she might wake confused. The fact that she didn't meant two things: one, she hadn't drunk enough gin the night before, and two, she would be all right. Beau was with her, but only as a sadness. It wasn't as if the planet had been ripped in half and suddenly there was no Africa.

She was safe, he was as safe as he could be, and there was nothing she could do. It was too early for coffee. With these thoughts, she drifted back to sleep.

It was the kettle that woke her later. The sun was properly up and Boris with it. Catherine remembered his news of the previous night and half smiled in her sleep; run of the mill days he would sleep on her couch until midday. A pretty girl smiles at him and he's suddenly a morning person. She bet herself breakfast that he would remark on how beautiful something was in the first fifteen minutes of the day.

'I mean, you think about it, we're mostly made of water, and so are clouds, it's like they're a part of us, just drifting without worries or rent, far above us.' Boris was on the balcony; staring at the sky and sipping coffee he had made for both of them.

'They're beautiful, aren't they?' Catherine smiled slowly to herself.

Boris kept looking at the cumulus clouds. 'Too right they are.'

Catherine had phoned the hospital and received the news that there was no news. She then spent two hours immersed in her usual life. She worked on the three pillbox blues and twice realised she hadn't thought of Beau in ten minutes. The plan for Philomena's green was behind her and she felt its presence. The steam and the colours began to mesh and she could see how this could possibly work. It was way off where it needed to be even for a prototype, but it was coming together.

How could the wild dogs have been in the same pen as Beau? The thought came unbidden. Catherine pushed it to the side, knowing it likely wouldn't help anyone.

The zoo lived and breathed safety. And would still. Just because there was an accident a few days after an elephant died didn't mean that there was anything wrong aside from bad luck and/or a mistake. To go there would be to meddle. To meddle would be unhelpful, to Beau, the zoo, and to her business, which really needed a success story or two from customers to keep afloat.

The people who will be watching us. Georgia's words at the hospital. Surely there was nothing here. But the way she had looked at her hands, Lady Macbeth in a pantsuit. It was just that Beau hadn't been popular and now was gone. It didn't usually happen in such a clinical way. Georgia hadn't been gloating at Beau's misfortune, but afraid for him. *And of all the people who would come looking.*

Catherine stood, stretching and reached for the hand cream that stopped her hands becoming as rough as a bricklayer. She stared up at Holly Golightly. There was an itch in the back of her brain that she wasn't going to ignore, even though right now she didn't want to think about it.

A text came through; Philomena: *I have found even on the worst days, hard work is the answer.*

Catherine paused at this. What on earth was going on? Why was this client, this lover of her enemy, sending such accurate and Calvinist messages? Catherine filed it in her brain under "bloody odd", and kept going.

The last pillbox done, she started on Philomena's green hat. The waves were too wide, which might look well on Philomena's striking features but would look comical on Grace's. Perhaps some form of cowl would look better, or wooden stocks perhaps? Catherine chided herself. School was a long time ago and she should be beyond this. The whole thing needed to be subtler. Perhaps with smaller waves, but a brighter colour she could…

Her phone rang and she jumped, a rare occurrence for her. She blinked twice at the name, partially obscured by the steam from her kettle. Philomena.

'This is Catherine.'

'Hello, Catherine, I have been feeling the most profound unease.'

Catherine licked her lips. 'You too, huh? I'm sorry to hear.'

'Have you begun on the hat?'

'Yes. I have.'

'Tell me truthfully, was that in that past eight minutes?'

Catherine breathed. There is nothing to fear in the truth unless you've hacked someone to death, right? 'Yes, that does seem scarily accurate.'

'I see.' Philomena took a moment. 'I should have warned you, when something is important I can know things about it even when I am not there.'

Catherine leaned back in her chair. 'How odd.' It was indeed the oddest thing that had happened to Catherine in a fortnight.

'My grandmother on my father's side had the gift as well. She was an Irish tinker from Ulster. I should have warned you.'

Catherine paused. 'Because this could make you seem…'

'Like a bizarre, witchcraft obsessed control freak.'

Catherine blinked again and cleared her throat, 'Not my words.'

A chuckle came down the phone. 'Nor mine, that's my ex.'

Catherine relaxed a little. 'Ah.'

'Don't fret, Catherine. I can't read your mind. I just get focused on things. The hat means so much to me.'

'For Grace.'

'For the Honourable Minister Chichester, yes. Without her I would not have secured my current post. It was as if she simply understood me and all I had to offer, as soon as we met. Have you ever experienced that, Catherine?'

Catherine consciously stopped biting her lip 'Once or twice.'

'Do you know Grace?'

'No,' Catherine said, faster than she should have.

'A remarkable woman.'

'I'll get on it, Philomena.' She hung up, in case Philomena wanted to tell her more. Her shoulders slumped. Managing customers' expectations was part of the job, but when they had a crystal ball, it could be excruciating.

For the next hour she crafted, moulded and stared at the felt form, her eyes going soft and then refocusing as her fingers pressed and aligned. If her brain was in three parts, one was on the hat, one was on Georgia's panicked words in the hospital and the third on Philomena's metaphorical magic mirror staring at her toil. It was more exhausting than it should have been.

At the same time, Georgia's words kept making her uncomfortable. Something wasn't at all right. She was sure that the police would sort it out. In the same way that climate change would be worked out, by a global community of the altruistic political class working in unison to–

That was enough. Mid-thought, her more curious and vengeful angels won out. She flicked the kettle iron off and went upstairs to get her coat.

As she walked the few steps to Anstey Station a man passed her, averting his eyes from her as she muttered, 'People don't mind who looks when there's nothing to hide.' Her phone vibrated. A text from Philomena: *I sense you are at a crossroads.* Catherine ignored it and kept walking as she saw a train coming in the distance.

Fourteen minutes later, Catherine was shocked to find a long queue waiting to get into the zoo. Whether this was a usual Wednesday crowd or whether Beau's attack had galvanised public interest, Catherine had no idea. She had been to the zoo only once previously in the past decade, and that was for evening drinks. There hadn't been any line then. Nor had there been so many children, who bounded and twitched right along the queue, surrounded by bored and irritable adults who were obviously filling in the hours before they could go and either drink heavily or scream into pillows. It was a frightening sight, a domestic holding port, and Catherine quickly walked away to the south side entrance.

On the east side, she noticed the staff entrance. The roller door opened to the side like a horizontal drawbridge to allow access to a man in khaki driving a BMW and gave Catherine a moment's clear sight into the courtyard, and what must have been office buildings of the staffing area. She was about to enter when she saw the crisp white shirt of a security guard who was standing just within the entrance and looking intently at her. Catherine smiled in what she hoped was a Canadian way and pointed to the south.

The south entrance was less crowded, possibly due to being further away from the train. After a few minutes wait Catherine found herself at a ticket booth where a woman of forty beamed at her from underneath a faded peroxide dye job.

'Member's card, please?'

Catherine blinked, 'Sorry?'

The attendant found still more teeth to display. 'I'm after your member's card, love.'

'Oh, I'm not a member.'

'Okey-dokey, admission for one then, card or cash?'

'Card is fine. I heard there was a mishap yesterday.'

'Ah, yeah. It's just awful. He's in hospital.' She didn't make eye contact. Possibly she was aware of the far-reaching conspiracy, possibly she was using the EFTPOS machine and had been asked the question seventeen times in the past half hour. Catherine chalked it up as an unknown unknown and walked towards the meerkat enclosure.

It was a stunning day. The sun shone in a late March way that made Catherine and others smile as they attempted to enjoy the benefits of the climate change that would make their grandchildren suffer so. Catherine moved past the meerkat enclosure, whose official opening she missed a few nights earlier, and walked as quickly as her legs and the Friends of the Zoo map could take her to the African wild dogs.

She shouldn't have been surprised to find the crowd was five deep, mostly adults, with many children trying to pull the grown-ups away. Police tape was visible beyond the enclosure, or what Catherine could see of it with such a horde around as she peered and overheard the conversations around her.

'I could have taken those little things, easy.'

'Nah, look at the teeth, he didn't stand a chance.'

'What a tit, getting caught in there with them.'

'Poor bastard.'

Catherine moved past, to the lions who were being paid no attention and were likely having a crisis of confidence. The enclosure had a walkway that went over the lions and wild dogs, and she took that, getting a better view than from the ground. She stopped in her tracks. There was a patch of ground that still had a bloody stain. It was wide, indicating either a struggle or damage to major arteries. It began very close to a door, not accessible to the public. Beyond that door was the police tape. She tried to remember times when she had seen that much blood and not a body. She couldn't remember many.

Catherine moved down the stairs, past the continuing throng near the wild dogs and wondered what to do next. She could try and find access to the staff quarters and get a feel for the place, or she could go to the gorilla enclosure and leave a flower on the rock. Both seemed to do Beau as much good as a sorer head. Perhaps she should just go and make hats and leave it to the police.

Then she saw a man she recognised, the angry drunk man Georgia had called Simon. He was reedy, with a mop of sandy hair and was now sober, or at least, not swaying. He was standing under an oak tree, simply watching the crowd. Instead of a tuxedo he wore keeper khaki, with a radio device on his hip, the same as Beau. He saw her looking at him and began walking away in the direction of the kangaroos.

'Hey,' Catherine called, friendly, but firm.

He kept walking.

'I said hey, Simon.' Firmer.

He stopped walking, turned around, gave a nervous smile.

'Hello?'

'You're a keeper.'

He was looking at her expectantly, with a hint of nervousness, in case she really did turn out to be an idiot. 'Um, yes?'

'I saw you two nights ago, at the party. You were yelling. I didn't realise you were a keeper.'

'Ah.' His face flushed in what appear to be sheer awkwardness. 'Oh God. I'm so sorry.' He ran fingers through his fringe, looked at his hand and then held it out. 'Simon.' He cringed as they shook hands. 'Which you know. Because you called me Simon. I really shouldn't drink. You are?'

'Catherine Kint. You're Simon Forster.' She was putting two and two together.

'Yes.'

'You worked on the trail team with Beau.'

Now he looked truly horrified. 'You know Beau?'

'Yes. He told me about you; said you would probably be doing Dong Zei's autopsy.'

He nodded, blushing less as they moved to a topic he knew about. 'Yeah, that's tomorrow.' He looked back at the dog's enclosure. 'I was just looking at the dogs. I can't believe it. I just can't see how.' He trailed off. 'You're a friend of his?'

'Yes.'

'Sorry.'

'You were saying you couldn't see how? You mean how the dogs would have got out of the enclosure.'

His cheeks went red again; the man went from a poised conversation to passing gallstones in seconds. 'I can't. We can't talk about it. There's been police. They'll be back. I'm sorry. I really have to…' He indicated with his walkie talkie.

'Just one question, Simon.'

'No, sorry.' His face was pained, but his intention was unmistakable as he turned and walked towards a staff area. Someone in a yellow t-shirt took her photo and gave her a thumbs up in a very touristy way.

Catherine moved back to the vantage from the ramp above the lion's enclosure. It gave no new answers, though the darkened ground made her swallow uncomfortably. Catherine wondered if she'd used the wrong tack. Perhaps she should have told him that he'd been charming company on Thursday. She doubted he would remember. A man behind her in a white shirt took her notice. Security. Catherine was sure he hadn't been there a minute earlier.

Catherine walked quickly across the promenade to the seals. She ducked past the bushes at their entrance and stepped back from the path, counting to fifteen in German. By *fünf*, Security was there, slowing his pace and pretending to be interested in something else.

She walked back to the promenade, he followed. Twenty metres behind.

So, Simon was rattled. So was the zoo, and she had a tail. A girl can take a hint.

Her phone rang as she passed through the south entrance, waving at the toothy attendant on the way out. Private number.

'This is Catherine.'

'It's me!' Female voice, not usually as enthusiastic as right now.

Catherine grinned. 'Britt! You sound excited. Are police officers allowed that much excitement?'

'I am.' Britt sounded like she was about to quietly burst.

Catherine could imagine her standing in a hallway, her face hurting with effort of suppressing a grin.

'I've made detective sergeant – I'm going to Homicide.'

'Yahoo! Blood and bodies and sleepless nights!' Catherine, of course, had no reason not to yell and so she bellowed across the zoo car park. 'Well done, Britt. Though now you're a detective you can't feel happiness. What would Williams think?'

'I'm just having a quiet moment. I called Dad, now you. I'll be dour in fifteen minutes, I swear.'

Catherine stopped walking to avoid being hit by a station wagon. A woman with a screaming baby glared at her. Catherine couldn't stop smiling. 'I'm so happy for you. When do you start?'

'In a few days. I'm just finishing up here at Robbery.'

'Go enjoy it, I'm sure there'll be a few noses out of joint.'

'Yep. They can kiss my well-paid arse.'

'Thatta girl.'

'Are you okay?'

'I'm having an interesting time, but call me about that later. This is your day, I shan't ruin it with mysteries we can't solve. Maybe tomorrow.'

'Okay. Talk soon.'

As Catherine walked towards Royal Parade she remembered Britt in the early years of their friendship as brash, confident, funny and ambitious. Catherine wondered if she had been drawn to her simply because she had ignored her own ambitions. Now in Homicide, Britt would be among the youngest women at that rank. Good for her, the world needed more glass ceilings smashed, even if it meant long days and nights. She would be hanging around with some of the most twisted individuals in Melbourne, and even if she got used to her colleagues, there were the crims.

There was a tram not far away, but on a whim Catherine kept walking towards the hospital. If nothing else, she wanted sympathy for her hard day, and in Beau's condition she knew he would be a good listener.

She entered the hospital and a cramp hit her abdomen – muscle memory. Without yesterday's adrenaline, it was less pleading with the gods and more a regret that benevolent deities weren't real. Good men are hard to find, good gods nigh impossible.

She took the lift to the fourth floor and walked to the intensive care unit. The clerk directed her to bed thirteen. She pulled the curtain and for a second was thrown again into pleading with absent gods. Beau was a pale body hooked up to breathing and heart rate monitors. The room was small and lit only by fluorescent lights, dominated by a machine beside him powering his lungs. His face was barely scratched, however, his chest was a mesh of bandages, some showing the red through them. There were deep and multiple defence wounds on both his arms. Catherine couldn't see his legs for the pale blue blanket that covered them, but could imagine they were badly injured.

'Oh honey, what did they do to you?' she said softly.

'Hello.'

Catherine jumped, and saw the nurse behind her. Her scrubs were dark brown; she was blond with kind, and very Germanic features, though her accent was pure west Melbourne.

Catherine pulled a hair past her ear. 'I'm sorry, I didn't see you.'

'No problem, I'm Belinda; I'm the nurse on for this shift with Beau. You are?'

'Catherine.'

Belinda's eyes went soft. 'Partner?'

Catherine coughed. 'No, just a lover.'

Belinda gave a small smile and checked some monitors.

'How are you holding up?' she asked, not looking away from a chart.

'I'm okay. How is he?'

She did look up then. 'We'll know more by tomorrow, I think.'

'There's,' Catherine looked apologetically at Beau's face, 'there's not a great deal of hope, is there?'

Belinda winced a little and didn't answer. After a minute she put down the chart. 'I've seen people do amazing things,' she replied at last. 'Patients you think have no hope walk away after two weeks. Others that you're sure will pull through just fade away in minutes.'

Catherine took Beau's hand in hers. His skin was very cool.

'How about, conventionally speaking, there isn't a great deal of hope?'

'Do you know much about chickens?'

Catherine thought she had been ready for any answer. Her forehead knotted.

'Um, taste good crumbed and with garlic?'

Belinda smiled while she continued checking dressings. 'Yes they do, and they do lots of other things. Do you know much about how the body of a chicken works? It's okay if you don't because other people do. Doctors, scientists and probably Beau here could tell you what every single part of the chicken's body does. The point I'm getting at is this – chickens we know, humans, we're learning more about all the time.'

'Right. We have the chickens nailed.'

'Well, no. I used to think that, but a doctor last week told me they've just found something new about chickens. Still, I like the thought.'

Catherine sat down. This was the kind of nurse you could spend some time with. 'Can I ask you about his wounds?'

Belinda was looking at them already, as she changed a dressing on his arm. She didn't look up. 'You'd probably get better answers from his doctors.'

'Are they here?'

She smiled. 'Not now.'

Then I'm asking you.'

'Okay.'

'What can you tell me?' Catherine was surprised at how small she sounded. She cleared her throat.

'The biggest problem was the gouging around his stomach and lower chest. He didn't fall down, despite having been attacked on all sides. There's significant defence wounds on his hands, his calves are a mess, as he had a couple on both of them. As he didn't fall, which I think is amazing, they didn't get near his face. I imagine most dogs would go for the face, but I'll ask Beau when he wakes up. There was damage to his oesophagus, stomach and liver, also a rupture to his pancreas and spleen. He's lucky that they didn't hit lower abdomen or his intestines would have fallen out. The biggest danger for him now is infection.'

Catherine's hand was gripping her own wrist so tightly that her fingers started to tingle. 'He put up a pretty good fight?'

'He's the only person I've nursed who was attacked by wild dogs but yes, he fought like a lion.'

Catherine stood, slowly. Belinda had finished her appraisal and was preparing to change a drip. Catherine went towards Beau, aware that she moved as he did not, aware he likely would not move again. She would have put a hand on his chest but it was thickly covered in the dressings, so she put a hand on his shoulder and saw again the bite marks on his arms.

'Good man,' she said quietly. His shoulder, like his hand, had barely any warmth. 'Keep fighting.'

The drinks had hardly been touched and they hadn't spoken for some time. Some nights were like that. Boris didn't mind.

'If I were six, Beau would have been the coolest person I ever met.'

Catherine looked up, smiled. 'How did he rate at your actual age?'

Boris stroked his beard. He looked up and noticed a small spider moving across the ceiling. 'Both times I served him a beer he seemed fine. Knew how to say please and thank you and didn't look at his phone while I was pouring the drinks.'

Catherine laughed sadly. 'You like that?'

'Waiting gracefully is a lost art.'

'Why do you say he would have been so cool, just the zoo-keeper thing?'

Boris propped himself up on an elbow. 'You mentioned that quiet confidence. A six-year-old is very aware of that. It's the age where you start to try, and it starts to hurt. Then you meet someone like Beau, who doesn't need to try to be confident and you think they have the world worked out. Then he's a freaking zoo-keeper.'

Boris took a sip, glad Catherine was smiling. 'I would have insisted he read me the bedtime stories.'

Catherine was quiet for a long time before saying, 'He seemed like a special guy.'

'He's still here.'

Catherine nodded grimly. 'And he may surprise me. I fear that if he can fight his way back to consciousness it would be a long way before he can work again. Or walk for that matter. Two nights ago, he was here, as alive as we are. Not breathing with a machine.'

'We're stardust. That's all.'

Catherine nodded, Boris continued. 'The only stardust we know of that's aware of itself, coming from the fertile ground and then re-joining it, one way or another. As fascinating as we are, whether we are dinosaur, ebola or octopus, we all end up compacted back into the energy of the planet.'

Catherine fought the tired urge to clap and simply poured another gin. Halfway through the talk she had got up. Boris was used to a moving target in a rant. 'And what do we do with this great if temporary gift?'

Boris raised his hands to each side. 'Try and be the boss, and mating. Always time for mating.'

Catherine smiled; it would sound sleazy from any other human. 'Tell me about the girl?'

He grinned, but shook his head. 'Later. It's not the night.'

Catherine raised an eyebrow, the gesture ruined as she stifled a yawn. 'I thought there was always time for mating?'

He shrugged, collecting the empties in front of him as he eyed the door. 'I was wrong, or maybe we're evolving.'

6

People who say 'I'm great with animals' are the same as people who say 'I'm great with kids', they're instantly untrustworthy.

~ Beau Hacska

In five more minutes, it would be 9.48am. Boris had walked more in his kitchen that morning than he did around the bar in a fortnight of double shifts. The tea towels in his shared house had borne witness to a frenetic pacing that Boris was only barely aware of. Had those rags of encrusted bio matter been able to speak – which was on the cards unless Boris put them through the wash sometime soon – they would have discussed the extreme mental anxiety this avuncular man put himself through anytime the prospect of romantic female company came up.

Of course, the tea towels had seen it all before, as had the pots, the chairs, the sink and of course, his housemates, who bore his tales of romantic dyslexia with varying degrees of patience, because he really was a good bloke and even washed the tea towels sometimes. They all had the same message: You want this too much. In fact, if the tea towels became verbal, their first utterances would be the word: "relax".

'See less of Catherine,' would probably be their first full sentence.

Hopeless romantic, emotional klutz, nice guy bringing up the rear and, of course, chunky – these were all the clichés he was quite happy with ninety per cent of his life. The only time it got his goat were days like this. Days when he knew he had to call a girl, and he knew, with aching certainty, that he was going to make a complete arse of it. The kitchen clock ticked over to 9.48. Show time. He checked that housemates were not in the vicinity. Nothing. He sighed again and made the call.

Ringing, ringing. Resisting the urge to hang up, to emigrate. The sun came from behind a cloud and illuminated the kitchen he had been pacing blearily for the past three hours. Surely it was a sign. More rings, Boris started pacing again.

'Hello.' The voice was bright.

'Hello, Melanie?' He knew it was her, she knew it was him. He had her name in his phone; he'd stared at it all morning.

'Molly.'

Boris stopped pacing, his back straight as a rod. 'What did I say?'

'Melanie.'

His eyes closed, slowly. 'Sorry.'

'Who is she?'

He blinked. 'Who?'

'Melanie, who is she?'

He blinked again, twice. 'What no. I don't. Um.' He moved forwards, steadying himself on the cold, steel structure of the stove. 'I don't know why I said that.'

'Do you wish you were speaking to Melanie?'

'No,' he half barked. 'Hold on.' He put the phone against his chest and breathed as deep as he possibly could, just as he and Catherine had discussed him doing any moment he was going completely to pieces.

He brought the phone back. 'Molly. Sorry. There were two girls called Melanie that I went to school with, one didn't speak any English for the first two terms and one called me fatty boomba when I was picked to be her partner in a bush dance. I have a second cousin called Melanie who is my cousin Ruth's daughter, she's five. Aside from those three I have no Melanies in my life though I quite like the *new pair of roller skates* song.'

There was a pause; Boris knew that Catherine would be counting in a language to pass the time. He couldn't pick a language – in fact he only knew English and Japanese for counting – but this silence had gone on well past an itchy knee.

It was then he could hear something like a pack of seals vomiting through a carpetbag, and realised that Molly was laughing, though concealing it.

'You're laughing.' He breathed. 'I really hope you're laughing.'

'Nice save Boris. You can call me Melanie if you need to.'

Boris sighed. 'First ball of the over. Wrong name, wow.'

'So there really isn't a Melanie?'

'Nor is there a Margaret, a Megan or a Nancy. My Mum's name is Mariah, I call her Mum.'

'Let's have dinner before you talk about your Mum.' Her tone had cooled, but Boris felt it was affected.

'Don't worry, I wasn't going to invite her.'

'Ah, thank God. So, are you free tonight?'

Boris' eyebrows lifted like they were expert pole-vaulters. Surely that was eager. 'I'm working tonight, free tomorrow?'

'Excellent. I do need to study tonight, but dinner with you was a more appealing prospect than mammal anaesthetic ratios.'

'I'm flattered, I think.'

'Don't be. Likewise, if I turn up at the bar tonight it's academia's failed allure, not your successful one.'

Boris caught sight of his own face in the window's reflection. He looked happy. 'As rivals go I will choose academia every time. So, you're doing vet?'

'Yep.'

'Tomorrow night, seven at your place?'

'It's a date.'

She paused, snorting softly. 'You just said that, didn't you?'

'And now I have my hand over my face.'

'Bye Boris.'

'Bye,' he paused, making sure, 'Molly.'

He sat in the kitchen for a few minutes before retreating to have a celebratory shower. The tea towels moved slightly in the breeze, although all the doors were closed.

Was it African grass? Was it African because it was tall? Or was it simply tall grass that was planted near the *Lycaon Pictus*, a.k.a. African wild dogs, so that children could see what it was like to walk a mile in the lycaon's shoes? Either way Catherine was now moving through the long grass to ascertain more about how Beau's accident had occurred. She was probably the first person to buy a membership so she could find out more about the locks. It occurred to her as she was doing it that in all her years of investigation, the culprit had never, ever been a locksmith. That seemed odd.

The locks in the reptile house were simply key and twist affairs. Several of the mammal enclosures had antechambers, presumably to keep the animals at bay – literally – while cages were maintained. Catherine hadn't been able to see the exact circumstances of the African wild dog enclosure, but was hoping this grassy path could lead to a vantage point.

She was rewarded at its most western point, where she could see a narrow maintenance trench that would logically lead to the dog's antechamber. Retrieving her small binoculars from her bag she surveyed the scene as best she could. The trench was wide enough for an adult and a half, or four dogs as needed, she supposed.

She swore quietly in Hindi as the vision went blurry, courtesy of a drop of Melbourne rain. Catherine had bet herself a wine at lunch that it would come down just as she found something interesting. She shook the binoculars and moved closer. There wasn't much to see, though if she stayed long enough she would be able to watch someone walk through it.

After five minutes the rain intensified, making Catherine repeatedly check her handbag for the rain poncho she was sure, absolutely sure, she had packed that morning. Now she imagined it, helpfully folded and placed next to the kettle on her kitchen bench.

The vibrating on her buttock told her the phone call had come. Philomena. Catherine ignored it. She had endured needy customers before. Psychic needy was a new level of irritation. As an antidote, Catherine visualised an air of productivity around her person, and hoped it was passed through the ether.

There was no movement in the trench. Catherine calculated that between feeds and maintenance, and people coming to check how the hell the locks had failed for Beau, there would be at least sixteen times when this trench would be used during the day. So, if you average out the twelve hours of daylight, at sixty minutes an hour, this would have to be used at an average of every forty-five minutes. She checked her watch. She had been watching for eight minutes, and was soaked. This was intolerable.

After a coffee under shelter she approached the first keeper she could see. She had been at the zoo for forty minutes and had seen no sign of security. She wasn't on the radar today and if asking a question got her on it, at least she'd get out of the rain. The keeper was about thirty, bespectacled, with chestnut hair pulled back in a severe ponytail, walking fast through the rain. Catherine approached from the side and spoke to her while keeping pace.

'Hello.'

The keeper turned her head, looking like an electrician who has been asked about plumbing. Catherine decided it was merely the rain that was annoying her and ploughed on.

'I'm Catherine, how are you?'

The keeper had the look of someone avoiding a salesman. 'Busy and wet.'

'It must be wonderful to work here.'

The keeper started walking perceptibly quicker. 'It's a joy.'

Catherine picked up the accent. 'Oh, you're from New Zealand, how long have you been here?'

'Long enough. I'm in a rush, do you have a specific question?'

Charm in the rain, like tits on a bull. 'I was thinking about the accident the other day and wanted to know how the locks worked.'

'I'm definitely in too much of a rush for that. Contact the police.'

Now she was almost sprinting, with Catherine moving gracefully in a side step motion to keep up.

'Do the doors have one or two locks?'

The keeper turned on her, eyes magnified by her wet glasses. 'He's a friend of mine.'

For a second they stood looking at each other in the rain. Catherine was aware of people watching them. She played her last card. 'Beau Hacska is my friend, too.'

She didn't blink as raindrops fell down her face. 'His name's in the papers.'

Catherine held her gaze. 'He's vegetarian. Drinks pale ale and smokes Champion Ruby but waits until everyone has finished eating.'

Something imperceptible passed over the woman's face.

'One lock.' Then she was gone.

Catherine walked slowly in the rain. The word of a keeper meant she was sure there was one lock, but could it have malfunctioned? Catherine was trained to rule out accidents or malfunctions before anything else. Many a case had dragged on with police exhaustively looking for motives, only to find that the victim slipped in the bath.

Catherine, noting the rain had eased, returned to her post in the tall grass. Between her and the trench was a two-metre glass wall which she tried to scale but wet glass was beyond even her superior climbing skills. She moved further around, away from the vantage point but unsure of what else she could do. It was then she heard a sound. Familiar, unmistakable and musical.

Breaking the Welsh tradition and belying the fact that it was March, was the Christmas carol *Ding-dong merrily on high.*

'Andy?'

The whistling paused, then continued but fainter, Catherine was almost thrashing to get out of the long grass, very nearly crashing into a damp Korean tourist who was smiling proudly in a photo as Catherine pushed past to get back to the main path. By the time she was in the open the whistling had either stopped or was no longer within earshot.

She moved away from the lion and dog enclosures to the open area. The rain had stopped; though dark clouds loomed like a threatening bouncer. The zoo seemed practically deserted; Catherine went on a hunch and stalked towards the north entrance. After a few paces she had given up. Even if it were Andy, what was he going to do aside from buy her lunch?

The whistling though, had seemed unmistakable. Even outdoors, whistling is an activity mostly frowned upon by anyone over the age of eleven, usually because it implies happiness and frivolity. Catherine thought it ridiculous that while in society it was perfectly acceptable to constantly play video games on a phone, never see a film that wasn't billed as "action" or live entirely on junk food, whistling was generally regarded as immature.

'Catherine?'

The phantom whistler himself was walking towards her from the direction of the little penguins. He was wearing, much to her delight, a pale shirt with "Zoos Victoria" printed on the left breast. He was clutching a clipboard and wore his usual bright expression. In fact, he looked delighted to see her. After the sullen Kiwi keeper, it was nice to be liked again. 'Did you call my name before? I thought I heard a lady's voice.'

Catherine couldn't help grin at his accent and the fact that the word "lady" didn't sound at all like an accusation. 'I did indeed, I was in the long grass and thought I heard your pucker.'

'Long grass, literally rather than metaphorically, I hope.'

'Yes.' She pointed. 'I was looking at the African wild dogs' enclosure.'

'Oh,' he sucked the side of his mouth. The black cloud now seemed to be directly over them. 'Terrible stuff there this week, did you hear?'

Catherine nodded a slow nod.

'Why are you here?' Andy's brow creased. 'Do you know him?'

'I do.'

'Was…?' It was Andy's turn to slowly nod, he used his whole head as he put two and two together. 'I met you, on the train after…Was Beau, Mr Bad Timing?'

Catherine smiled sadly. 'Up until the other day you were Mr Bad Timing, he had the right timing.'

He whistled and inhaled. 'Shite, poor bastard. Wow. Beau. Small world, eh?'

'You know him well?'

He shook his head. 'No, we spoke once. I work in admin. The keepers don't have much use talking to me. Though, I happen to have a hobby studying frogs.' He puffed up a bit as he said it.

'That must keep you up at night.'

He smiled. 'I like them, always have. So, when a job came up here I left the bank and I've been here four years.'

Catherine began walking the way Andy had been going, Andy fell into a languid step. 'Can you tell me anything about the accident?'

He was quiet a minute. The sun had come out and the wet bitumen was steaming. It was beautiful. 'Um, sure, but why?'

'A few things I've been told don't seem to make much sense. I thought I'd have a look around here.'

'Aren't you a milliner?' The rain started again. Andy didn't seem to notice, aside from pulling his clipboard closer to his chest.

'One of the best in Melbourne, according to my website.'

It turned out Andy was on his lunch break, quite happy to share it with her, and knew which vendor sold the best food. A hop, step and a sandwich later and Catherine couldn't believe her luck. Until he said this:

'I know next to nothing about zoo procedure unless it involves a spreadsheet. Or a tree frog.'

Suddenly Catherine could again believe her luck. It was higher than Beau's, higher than many in the world, but still well below the median luck index for humanity. Andy caught her look.

'Sorry.'

Catherine nodded the look away. 'Let me try. People often know more than they think they do.'

Andy drained his coffee and brushed a crumb off his beard. His eyes were intent on her.

Catherine put her hands together, pressing in concentration. 'Prior to Tuesday's incident, have there been any major mishaps in the time that you've worked in the zoo?'

'An orangutan escaped one day. He was caught without incident, though he did steal a vegemite sandwich.'

'Right. The lock systems on most enclosures have one lock, correct?'

'I have no idea.'

'Do keepers generally work solo or in a team?'

'I think it varies, I'm not sure.'

'What emphasis on safety is there in the zoo environment?'

'I've got that one. The zoo is heavy on safety, with two full day's training given to all staff and volunteers. Roughly half of that is around dealing with mental illness – the zoo has a high instance of mentally ill customers. You might recall in the '80s a fellow climbed the lions' den walls after hours wearing only his black belt.'

Andy made a face that spanned four emotions in the space of two seconds. 'The other parts of the training are in the unlikely event of mishap and of course the procedures that stop mishaps from occurring. It's a very thorough course. With refreshers, every year.'

'See, you do know more than you thought.'

He winced. 'It's hardly helpful though. Health and Safety always has a big focus in any organisation with more than twelve staff. I'm sure the National Australia Bank has a similar course, they just substitute the word python for stress, or arithmetic fatigue.'

Catherine looked at him flatly. 'Arithmetic fatigue?'

He winced again. 'I really hated working in the bank.'

Her voice did not change. 'Arithmetic fatigue?'

'Just because I had the only case ever recorded doesn't make it made up.'

'Right.' She couldn't help but like him. She knew lots of people who worked in banks, generally the more they hated it the more she liked them. Extra points if they never considered buying a salmon coloured shirt or sunglasses where the brand was bigger than the lens.

Anyway,' he continued, 'what I mean is, I haven't told you anything useful. Though I'm happy to look out for things for you.'

Catherine leaned back slightly, scratching her back on the wooden chair. 'Very kind. Why?'

He shrugged. 'You appreciate whistling. It's rare.' He shuffled in his seat. 'What should I look for, dodgy deals? Ivory smuggling?'

'No, nothing like that. I can't see why the zoo would try and smuggle ivory when there's people who kill elephants quite cheaply over in Africa. Just keep your eyes open. I'm not even sure what I'm looking for yet. It could have been an illness that killed Dong Zei and an accident that hurt Beau.'

Andy was slightly crestfallen. 'I was hoping for some derring-do.'

'Just focus on your access to frogs.' She paused. 'Where are the frogs here?'

'They're connected to the reptile house.'

'You know I've never been there' She brightened 'Thanks.'

'Well, okay.' He did light up a little every time he thought about frogs. Catherine hoped that hats still did that for her.

She fingered a sugar satchel thoughtfully. 'I have one job that you can go on with.'

He leaned forward.

Catherine was momentarily distracted by a family singing happy birthday to a tubby four-year-old. When she looked back, Andy was still attentively looking at her. 'Try and find out who was first on the scene when Beau was attacked.'

'Oh, that's easy. The worst kept secret in the place.'

'Who?'

'Ian Bradbury.'

As long as Catherine could remember television, she could remember Ian Bradbury with a Yorkshire accent waxing lyrically on fish or finches, kestrels or crabs. Of course, it wasn't the first time she had met someone well known, but investigating a celebrity was new. It was unavoidable though. Ian was first on the scene of what was potentially an attempted murder. Catherine knew that as an adult with a cat, a business, taxes and a washing line, she could make the disconnection with the fantasy of television. Her inner child, however, did feel like she was about to investigate Superman.

These thoughts accompanied her into the St Vincent's intensive care unit. She smiled as she entered the room and found not only Beau's nurse Belinda, but the figure of Georgia Potter. One noticed her, did one not?

'Just give me an indication, what percentage is the chance of a full recovery?'

'Somewhere between five and fifty per cent, there's so much unknown here. He's stable, but there's no way of knowing if he'll recover or if he lost too much blood initially for his brain to be able to function at its normal level again.'

Belinda looked over Georgia's shoulder and nodded to Catherine. 'Hi Catherine.'

Georgia turned slowly, like she was about to see a ghost.

Catherine gave her a wink. 'Hedging a bet?'

Georgia looked stung.

Catherine was unsure as to why, and moved on. 'So no change then?'

Belinda shook her head. 'Same as yesterday. There's hope, but not an abundance.'

Catherine noticed the diminished shock of seeing Beau unconscious. It was probably for the best that she wasn't falling apart, but it seemed mercenary. It was hardly Beau's fault that his conversation had been rubbish for a few days.

Belinda obviously felt the temperature in the room drop and excused herself, saying she would return in two minutes. After she left, Catherine stared at Georgia, who in turn stared at Beau.

Catherine broke the ice. 'You didn't tell me that Ian Bradbury was the first on the scene.'

Georgia made no eye contact. 'Why would I have told you that?'

'Because you know I'll find out eventually.'

'I don't know all that much about you, Catherine.'

'How is he?'

'You heard. '

'Not Beau; Bradbury.'

'He's fine. Of course.' She paused, swallowed. 'I have been cooperating with the police in full. I don't know why I need to point that out.'

'I didn't think you were criminal, Georgia, or stupid. I need to know what happened and you blocking me has become conspicuous.' She attempted eye contact. 'I can help.'

Georgia continued looking at Beau. 'I'm fighting a battle on three fronts right now, Catherine. You could help by not creating a fourth. Also, I'm not blocking you. You're not investigating this accident, you're a milliner.'

Catherine held up two fingers. 'Beau asked me to investigate something,' she lowered one finger. 'Now he's in ICU. It ups the stakes, but you're not in the frame. Though while you're here, where were you when you found out about this?'

Georgia rounded on her, spitting words. 'You can dig. Dig as much as you like. You're not going to like what you find. There's only one way those dogs got out.' As soon as she stopped she winced.

Catherine stepped forward. 'Go ahead.'

Georgia began shutting down. 'No, I shouldn't have. I'm sorry.'

'He would want me to know.'

Georgia shook her head, almost whispering. 'I don't think he would.'

Catherine took a deep breath and thought about the possibilities that Beau wouldn't want her to know. They were hardly at the infidelity stage, bestiality wasn't plausible, and being a Neil Diamond fan was inconceivable. Which left one thing: 'You think it was suicide.'

Georgia bit her lip. Her eyes were sympathetic. Catherine's head tilted. 'And you believe it.'

Georgia's lips were trembling. 'I'm sorry.'

'You're wrong.'

'I couldn't believe it, either.'

Catherine's voice was flat. 'You're wrong.'

Hours later, in her studio, Catherine tried to focus completely on the green felt in front of her and ignore her guts, which were as twisted as a tobacco lobbyist. Her thoughts were circular and she was trying to ignore them, too. She was trying to view the hat in front of her and forget about who was going to wear it. The idea of Beau deliberately hurting himself was abhorrent and ridiculous. She rejected that idea strongly but then came the doubt, like a terrible aftertaste.

The thought that she could have been wrong followed. That someone could spend a night with her and decide to end it all a few hours later. Then the rejection came again, but it was that mid-point doubt that was gnawing at her. She felt dirty for considering it.

Then she would remember the scar on his wrist, rejecting that too. The guy worked with animals. Lots of scope for scars.

She remembered him talking about feeling trapped by the accusations. She remembered that she barely knew him at all.

The bloody hat was going nowhere.

Music did not sufficiently distract her, and then tea did nothing. Catherine could tell that this problem would not even be helped by gin. So, after another futile hour of trying not to worry, action became the only possible remedy.

She had almost expected the phone to go when the buzz came through. Catherine didn't look at who was calling, but answered.

'This is Catherine.'

'Hello Catherine. I sense you're working hard.'

'Philomena, I am.'

'Do you find me calling a distraction? I have faith, but this hat is of great importance to me and I sense you are conflicted.' She paused. 'You have had a death, no?'

Catherine leaned back in her chair. She had half prepared this. 'Philomena, I have, though that's not something that you would have ever known in the usual run of things. I assure you I have gone through lots and still fulfilled what a client needs. You say you have faith, can I ask that you show it through respectful radio silence?'

'I know it is rude. However, I am paying and suspect that you have had worse clients in the past.'

'Is that a sense?'

Philomena grunted. 'No, I'm a fifty-year-old woman, I know how the world works.'

Catherine's eyebrow twitched. 'Well, there you have me. You're not even close to the worst.' She looked at the hat, wondering again if she could allow for a slow release poison in it for Grace.

'Can you tell me why you are conflicted? Is it the death?'

Catherine's eyes widened. 'Just infinite curiosity in a finite world, Philomena. The hat will be done by Wednesday, I assure you. Goodbye.'

Catherine breathed deeply. Perhaps a gin would help after all.

Behind every crime is a reason. If Beau hadn't tried to hurt himself, and an accident seemed less and less likely, this was a crime, with money, power or revenge behind it. Lust was also a possibility, but she couldn't come to that just yet.

Hence at the hour of twenty minutes past two, Catherine called the all singing, all dancing and all hacking money-follower, Nealamber Singh.

'Catherine! Hello.'

'Hello indeed! You wonderful fellow.'

Catherine closed her eyes as Neal went into peals of laughter.

'Yes, I do need something,' she said into the receiver, holding the phone away from her face.

'I thought so,' he replied.

Catherine imagined him taking the neatly folded handkerchief out of his ironed breast pocket and dabbing fastidiously at his eyes as he grinned into the ether. Neal had been helping her for years and no task had ever been too difficult. Yet Catherine didn't ring him much unless she needed a favour. It wasn't that she took him for granted, she was just busy. Then when she did call, he always laughed it off and took it in his stride. He was an enabler for her poor social skills.

'What's the job, and are you well?' His cheerful voice held all its usual warmth, good humour and Punjabi accent.

'The job is the zoo, and I am middling.'

Neal gave an intake of breath. 'Troubled times at that place this week. Are you involved?'

'I'm afraid so. The unfortunate elephant was being treated by the unfortunate keeper, with whom I was, as you say, involved.'

'Ahh.' He paused, full of sympathy, and Catherine was filled with a warmth she hadn't realised she needed. 'I am sorry. What's his prognosis?'

Catherine looked around her desk, wondering if she had known him longer would Beau's photo have adorned part of it. 'It's not good.'

'I see. So, is your interest due to his accident?'

'In part. He had asked for help with the elephant investigation. They were pinning all responsibility on him. I want to make sure everything is kosher in the zoo's books. I don't trust the chairwoman of the board at all.'

'Her name?'

'Georgia Potter.'

'I'll look her up as well.'

As she knew he would. 'You're a brick, Neal. How are you? Has June arrived?' Catherine remembered Neal's fiancée was due to join him in Melbourne having completed her doctorate through Bangalore University.

'Yes, she flew in last month. And aside from being happy all the time we're coping just fine, thank you.'

A slow grin moved over Catherine's face. 'So, no re-entry problems?'

His voice raised in volume and pitch. 'I shall not dignify that with any kind of response. Call me in three days if I haven't called you with some findings.'

'You're the best Neal.'

'So I'm told.'

Fifteen minutes later, Catherine had switched to rock music and the hat was actually taking shape. Nothing ever moved tension in her gut like action, even if that was just getting Neal to take action. While she moved the fabric in her hands she began to see how it would look on Grace, how the green would contrast with her pale skin. If she was forced to make her enemy beautiful then let her enemy know it was her, and hopefully hate her for it.

It would be striking, and if she could get the angles right it would resemble the sails of a schooner.

Another half hour and the hat had progressed no further. Also, the satisfaction from getting someone else to do something had worn off. There is action, then there is delegation; and delegation wasn't going to cut it for long today.

The zoo's switchboard had turned her onto Ian Bradbury's own website for contact details. The supplied phone number was international. She called the number and left the message that she was a friend of Beau Hacska's and wanted to talk to him about the accident. She assumed she wouldn't get a call back.

Time to get aggressive.

'Hello, market and compliance, Andy speaking.' His Scots accent was even more muted over the phone, which Catherine found depressing.

'This is your favourite milliner.'

'Ah, hold on.' He paused, 'No, I don't know any other milliners, so yes you are.' The accent was stronger as soon as he knew who it was. Catherine wondered if it was a sign of empathy or weak will.

'I need a favour.'

'Ask away.'

'If I wanted a cup of tea with an Englishman who works at the zoo, could you help?'

He was silent for a full two seconds. 'I'm not English.'

'Ian Bradbury is.'

'Ah.' He paused. 'You want a lead.'

'I need to talk to him.'

He cleared his throat, spoke quietly. 'I don't have access to his file.'

Catherine gripped her desk. 'Can you get it?'

'Christ no, but I know he has a view of Poplar Oval.'

'What's that?'

'A cricket oval in Royal Park. It's above the train line. I've seen him around there when I've had football training, and I spoke to him about it. How's that?'

'I can work with that. Thanks.'

'Hey. Wait.'

'What?'

'How about a cup of tea with a Scotsman?'

Catherine's face creased. 'Timing's improving, but still not quite there. Don't worry, I'm sure I'll call again.'

He groaned. 'I'm counting the seconds, I assure you.'

Catherine hung up the phone. She decided Boris would quite like Andy.

It was after four by the time she was near the oval at Royal Park. This was an older part of town, close to the zoo and gardens, leafy and quiet. It was beautiful in the afternoon light. Catherine walked the streets looking for signs of a zoological broadcasting genius. She looked into gardens for likely lodgings, discounting anything that had children's play equipment. She also checked cars for tell-tale signs of a lifetime spent with animals, like an ivory tusk in the back seat or a hippo tooth on the dash. She kicked her heels. This was a long shot.

A vibration started in her buttock, she took her phone out of her pocket and almost hurled the thing into the nearest cricket oval. Philomena. Catherine could imagine her meditating on the hat and Ayn Rand. The text reported: *You are wasting hat-making time and your own precious seconds on Planet Earth.*

Catherine gave a verbal response to the wind. 'Yes, Philomena. Quite right and well done. Doesn't mean we need to talk about it. Don't you think?' Catherine silenced the phone and kept looking.

She knocked on the doors of three houses with cars parked out front that sported "Friends of the Zoo" stickers. No Ians, though one chap offered to be "Ian" if it meant she would stay. Catherine gave him a look that would curdle milk and was tempted to steal his garden gnome.

She stopped outside number 39 Poplar Road, staring at the car. A black Subaru Forester, immaculately clean, with a cream polo sweater on the back seat. The car was suitable for drives to the country, elegant, not flashy but not cheap. A quick viewing of the boot showed a brown bag with a stethoscope, a protractor and what looked like a discarded crisp packet. Expensive things to leave in the car, even in this gentrified neighbourhood.

The path up to the door was well tended but not meticulous. The garden seemed low maintenance. Perfect digs for the temporarily boarding international celebrity, or else Catherine was simply seeing what she wanted to see. She rang the bell, a low ring that made Catherine think the butler would answer presently. In effect, no one did, and after three rings Catherine shouldered her handbag and moved back to the street. Only to come face to face at the gate with Ian Bradbury, carrying a litre carton of milk and a packet of chocolate biscuits.

'Hello.' His face showed that he recognised her, but not the details.

'Hello Ian, I'm Catherine Kint, we met last week at the meerkat opening.'

He smiled. 'Oh yes! How are you?'

Catherine smiled without trying. It was so nice to have a voice from childhood finally directly addressing her. 'I'm well. I was hoping to have a talk with you.'

He slowed. 'What do you do again?'

'I'm a milliner. But that's not why I'm here. I want to talk to you.'

'About?'

'I was hoping you could tell me more about the Sumatran tigers.'

His eyebrows knitted, then he smiled and held up the biscuits. 'Tea?'

'Lovely.'

The house was elegant if sparsely furnished. While Ian made the tea, and chatted to her from the kitchen she looked around the lounge room. There were five photos on the mantelpiece: one of Ian with the Secretary-General of the UN, one of Ian with a young man on his graduation day and three separate photos of a young girl, about twelve years old. Then a photo of the same girl, but now almost Catherine's age.

A series of letters were piled on one side, unopened, seemingly forwarded from the Ian Bradbury Foundation. Fan mail perhaps. And the silver foil of a medication. The pill packet was half empty – Donepezil.

'Do you take sugar?'

Catherine sat down on the armchair in front of the coffee table. 'White and one, thank you Ian.'

'I don't wear hats much, I'm afraid.'

'It's a shame. As clichéd as it sounds, you'd pull off a bowler.'

'With a feather, I hope?'

'One that's taken as a gift, humanely too.'

He laughed, putting the tea on the small table and sat down on the arm of the chair Catherine sat in. He leaned close. 'Did you really want to talk to an old man about hats?'

Catherine stayed perfectly still. 'No. About Beau.'

His face shadowed. 'I thought it was tigers.'

'We may get to them. Mostly I wanted to talk about Beau.'

He sat on the couch across from her, dejectedly reaching for his tea. 'A friend of yours?'

'Yes. I wanted to talk about the accident.'

'The accident.' The side of his mouth twitched. 'You mean the dogs?'

'Why don't we start at the elephant, Dong Zei?'

He swallowed his tea and was quiet for a moment. 'Catherine, you're a milliner not a journalist?'

'Yes, I'm a milliner. Though I do investigate things when people ask me to.' She sipped her tea and watched him absorb this. 'Never for print.'

He looked at her over his cup, not moving. Catherine was about to speak when he did.

'Do you know much about elephants?'

Catherine leaned back. 'I've had a crash course in the past few days, some fascinating reading, but more fascinating was how much guess-work there seems to be in the diagnosis and treatment of them. Some of the protocols I found actually said...'

'Give a slightly higher dosage than you would a horse,' he countered.

'Right.'

'Well, yes I see you've done some homework.' He crunched on a biscuit. 'Tell me, have you read about EEHV?'

It rang a bell. 'Elephant Endo.'

Her memory failed her, but Ian looked delighted. 'Yes, you're almost there. Elephant Endtheliotropic Herpes Virus.'

'If I'd had seven more goes,' she smiled, 'I'd still be nowhere.'

Ian laughed and ate another biscuit.

'The language is a challenge to newcomers, no question. EEHV is extremely serious in Asian elephants such as Dong Zei. It involves very quick internal bleeding. If the virus reaches the heart, well, there's nothing that can be done.'

For the first time, Beau's allegation that Dong Zei previously had been in robust health seemed irrelevant.

'So it made sense that Beau didn't diagnose this early?'

'You said he was a friend of yours?'

Catherine nodded.

Ian leaned forward in his chair, his hands together. Catherine noticed his knuckles were white.

'Yes. You were first on the scene?'

'With Dong Zei?'

'The dogs, the accident.'

'I was.' He blinked twice. His knuckles again turning white.

'I'm sorry to bring it up, but it's important for me to understand. Beau was more than a friend.'

He nodded, seemingly steeling himself. 'Well. I can tell you I was on my way to the elephants.' His voice was quiet, but strong. 'When I looked through to the wild dogs I had the feeling something was wrong for about a minute when I heard a scream. It was Beau. Being early in the morning there wasn't anyone around.'

He picked up his tea, then put it down again.

'I moved to the keepers' access and ran for the door. I found some beef that was going to be used as the lion's meal for the day and opened the door. The dogs then split, with half of them staying on Beau, who had kept his feet somehow and the other half towards me, I threw the beef as far as I could.

'The dogs are pack animals, and when those that were coming at me peeled off as a group to go after the meal I was able to grab Beau and pull him to the keeper's area. The door locked,' he looked at her pointedly, 'easily. From there, I radioed for help.'

Catherine was amazed. It sounded like one of the greatest acts of heroism she had heard of.

'And no one saw this?'

'No. Thankfully. Beau was covered in blood.' He looked up from his hands. 'I'm sorry, are you okay to hear this?'

Catherine nodded, ignoring the dryness in her mouth.

'He must have known that if he'd fallen they would have ripped out his throat,' Bradbury said. 'He was exhausted. I'm sure that in moving him I likely did more damage, but if I had left him in there, well...'

'So, when you opened the door, it came easily?'

'Yes, I had the key. I'm afraid to say, the lock was in perfect working order.'

'Did Beau say anything?'

Ian looked at her for a long time. 'I'm not sure I should say any more. Catherine, I spoke to the police already.'

He reached for his tea.

Catherine caught his wrist. 'He spent the night before with me. He was uncomfortable with some things that were happening. I need to know what he said.'

Ian pulled his hand away and Catherine let it go. He took out a handkerchief and wiped his face, dabbing his eye. 'He said thank you.'

Catherine's voice caught in her throat. A stream of air blowing out her nose. 'That's all?'

'That's all. He passed out as he said it.'

'Do you think it was suicide?'

The room was getting darker as the sun began to lower.

He shook his head. 'He must have fought them for five minutes at least. I didn't think suicides fought like that.'

'Me neither.'

They were quiet a minute. Ian rubbed the side of his face. 'You said he was, um, uncomfortable about the business at work?'

'Yes, regarding Dong Zei.'

'I see.' He reached for his tea again, finished it.

'Ian, I do appreciate this. Tell me, is there anyone else who you saw in the vicinity?'

He stared at the carpet, lost in thought.

The bell rang. Ian looked up. 'Ah, that will be Simon.' He winced as he stood up.

Catherine finished her tea.

Simon came in with his thin frame bent over, staring at her. Switched on a light, which made both Catherine and Ian blink.

Simon's eyes were cold. 'What is she doing here?'

He stared at Ian, his voice flat.

'Simon, this is Catherine.'

'I know. Why is she here?' His voice was higher than Catherine remembered it.

Ian's hand was touching Simon's shoulder, so lightly. 'We're just talking about hats, Simon.'

Simon took a deep breath, swallowed. 'Of course. Course you were.'

'It's all right, son. Nothing to worry about.'

Simon shook his head. 'Yep. Got it.'

Ian looked at Catherine, who was already standing.

'Remember Ian, a bowler is the one for you.'

'I'll consider it,' he said carefully.

Ian and Simon were whispering intently as she let herself out, though she couldn't make out the words.

7

You want people to hate you? Just be happy at work.
Even the most cheerful of them will assume you're stealing the paperclips.
~ Andy McCafferty

Catherine had enough time to smoke a cigarette before Simon emerged. Of course, she didn't smoke one, but as a private detective who respects the classics it was the amount of time she was going to wait before going home. He walked past her perch near a large peppercorn tree and strode out to the ovals in the general direction, Catherine was pleased to see, of the zoo.

She walked fast behind him. As she came within three metres he turned and grimaced at her. 'Oh, hello.' His tone was normal, though his voice seemed to regularly break.

'You're in a hurry again,' Catherine noted.

'I remembered something I had to do. Ian will join me later.' He quickened his pace.

Catherine had to trot to keep up. 'I'll walk with you.'

'I walk fast.'

Catherine had noticed, but pretended not to. 'How did you meet?'

'Working in South Africa.'

'When.'

The pace increased. 'Seven years ago. Why?'

'You seem comfortable with each other, but very different.'

His hands were in his pockets, amazing for the speed his legs produced. 'I look out for him.'

'How?'

'Women,' he said, almost imperceptibly.

'What?'

'Nothing.'

Catherine quickened to see his face. 'You said women, didn't you?'

'Um.' He was walking faster, looking at her sideways. 'It's um, none of your business?' It was one of those statements that shouldn't have been a question, but his tone implied it.

'Where were you on Monday morning?' Catherine was having trouble keeping her breath normal.

'You're not serious,' he said quietly.

'I'm seriously asking. Ian's first on the scene, confronts death, where are you?' Catherine was beginning to get a stitch.

'I lecture on Mondays.'

'You what?'

'Lecture,' he stopped so suddenly that Catherine would have been intimidated if she wasn't so wheezingly grateful.

'I lecture, Catherine. Zoology. Three days a week. Monday is one of them. Will you excuse me? I really have to get on.'

He was back to an Olympic pace and Catherine had barely begun to control her breath again.

She followed at a distance. In her mind's eye the view of her gym membership gathering dust on the top of her fridge made her cringe. Simon must be a fitness freak, she decided, a gymnast or triathlon enthusiast in his spare time. Though he too had slowed down and was only two hundred metres ahead of her. He didn't look back as he entered through the staff doors.

Catherine breathed deeply three times and then jogged the remaining distance to the customer gates, flashing her newly acquired zoo membership through the gate.

'We're only open another forty-five minutes,' the attendant told her.

'All I need,' Catherine murmured, channelling her inner tree frog enthusiast.

She moved quickly to stand underneath the large oak tree that gave the best view of the main promenade. Assuming Simon wasn't staying in the staff section, she guessed he would move toward the elephants and this would provide her the best spot to see. She counted to twelve and he appeared. Still hunched, though his pace had reduced from warp speed to the same pace as visitors, with shoulders hunched and his head forward.

He wasn't moving towards the elephants, but towards the reptile house. As he passed her he moved faster, at first to avoid a family of visitors, though he continued briskly and Catherine wondered if she had been spotted.

She followed, exposed, at a distance of fifty metres, running as he entered. She stopped outside the entrance to avoid running in and making the tailing more obvious than it needed to be. It was a good move; he had only moved a few metres to the left.

The reptile house is a looping darkened tunnel with illuminated windows on either wall, housing dozens of the world's most amazing reptiles. The effect is beautiful. It is a still place, the reptiles mostly slow moving, and the dark brings silence, whether accidentally or by design.

As she watched, Simon moved slowly, pausing at each window for twenty seconds. Catherine followed from eight metres back, keeping as far from the lighted windows as she could. As he walked through the house, his poise began to change. His head moved back, she could see him breathing deeply. At a crocodile enclosure, he paused for a long time. He stroked the glass gently.

After about thirty seconds she saw him put his hand in his pocket. He brought something out and held it, rubbing it between his fingers. Catherine risked a step closer, and stifled a grunt as she stepped into a small girl with blonde hair. Off balance, Catherine had to lurch to her right, very nearly breaking the glass enclosing the Western Australian legless lizard. Miraculously the girl hadn't squealed, but looked both apologetic and delighted with herself. Her hand was at her chin as she gave a gap-toothed grin.

Catherine brought a finger up to her lips to keep the girl quiet. She nodded, and Catherine went back to her vigil. Simon was still moving his hand; Catherine thought perhaps there was a string connecting the object to his belt.

'Eliza.' A woman's sharp voice rang through the darkened house, many heads lifted. The small girl moved towards a dark-haired woman. When Catherine looked up, Simon was walking, faster than ever, through the muted light towards the exit.

At eight in the evening, Catherine was pleased to be still working on a hat. She wasn't even thinking of finishing. She was working. On a hat. Like a grown-up, a sober grown-up at that. For some reason, she thought Beau would have approved rather than been disappointed. Philomena, she hoped, was serenely cooing somewhere in the leafy suburbs.

The hat worked on six out of eight angles. She was closing in.

Though there was no time to celebrate. A hat worked from all angles or it didn't work at all. If it looked bad from one side, that was the side it would be noticed.

Catherine wiped the block and inhaled deeply before starting again.

As she worked, her mind kept wandering back to the crucial words that Bradbury had said – 'I had the key, it was easy.'

Someone had let the dogs loose, or she had completely misjudged Beau. It had happened before, sometimes she was wrong. Yet it seemed inconceivable. Suicidal people don't have extra pints the night before, or at least not so happily.

She was going to have to see that door, at all its angles. Bradbury had said that there was hardly anyone around at that time. Perhaps she would set an alarm tomorrow. She looked at the clock – eight-twenty and still working and thinking about setting an alarm. This was the old Catherine talking.

She paused and found she was happy, or at least content, and that made it okay. Hard work is fine, provided you're enjoying it.

'It was easy, I had the key.' The soundbite continued, then he went on to his description of Beau fighting the dogs, of the blood.

Then Forster came to mind, yelling about Beau's incompetence.

Someone had killed him, or wanted to hurt him at least, she was ninety per cent sure of it. Which was just sure enough to get very, very angry.

The fact that all the major suspects were "animal people" only confirmed that it was a murder attempt. A zoologist knows what an animal can do.

Of all the people she'd met in the past week, no one seemed strange or twisted enough to hurt someone and not think about it. It was the usual tapestry of flawed and normal human beings, even the famous one.

Simon was clearly odd, though sharp. There was something in the way Ian Bradbury had spoken to him, almost a pleading that made Catherine think that either Ian Bradbury was the peacemaker, or that Simon had reason to be annoyed. Perhaps it was explained in his muttering about women. Ian was certainly game.

At the meerkat opening, Simon had seemed, for a moment, deranged enough to hurt someone. If he believed that Beau was responsible for Dong Zei's death, then it gave him a motive.

Georgia's vigil at Beau's bed troubled her as well. Catherine wondered what her whereabouts were on Tuesday. Beau was opinionated, strong willed and respectful in his disagreement. That was worse for some managers than a frothing lunatic. As a motivation, it was slim, but she had seen people killed for less.

Was Georgia visiting Beau in the hope he would recover? Or not?

Ian Bradbury's story needed to be checked, and Georgia would be the first port of call. Or perhaps Andy. Even if it had been kept out of the papers, there would be gossip in the zoo community. It would be as reliable as any gossip, but any information is better than none.

With that, she downed tools, poured a drink and turned on the stereo. She looked out the window. Outside was a world, in the world was the pub. She turned the possibility over, and decided not to. On a scale of one to ten, she felt exhausted. If she was going to get through half of what she needed to tomorrow, she would need to be up early. She set the alarm.

The next morning, sunlight spilled into Catherine's lounge room in what should have been a pleasant experience. Adversely, it had been forty-five of the most frustrating minutes of Catherine's life. Forty-five minutes she could have spent working, bushwalking, in the bath or talking to Boris. Yet she was here. In front of a computer screen, searching though the website of a university that she wasn't a student of.

It was soul destroying.

A quick internet search had identified Simon Forster as being an "experienced and brilliant zoologist temporarily living in Melbourne and augmenting our program" with the University of Melbourne. One of the two universities Catherine had studied in, Melbourne Uni is a sprawling elegant behemoth of a campus just an elite discus throw from the Melbourne Zoo grounds. It made sense that Simon would moonlight there. This initial investigative success made Catherine want to ring Neal and brag about her improving brilliance with research. This feeling soon soured, as she found herself jumping through multiple hoops with no success.

First, she had attempted to find out information regarding zoology subjects and lecturing times through the faculty's specific page, spending more time than she would like to admit pressing "update" on an obviously obsolete page, before realising that their listed Christmas breaks were for a previous year. She then spent ten minutes learning about the new "student portal" and its ground-breaking "one stop shop" approach to the complexities of university life. By the time Catherine's tea had gone cold, she was seriously questioning the evolutionary process that took humanity to this point of exponentially complicated information sharing.

As a workaround, she enrolled – somewhat easily – as Boris Shakhovskoy and began looking through to lecture times, only to find they had not been uploaded. The site directed her to the student noticeboard. This noticeboard, for all the information she could find about it, could have been in one of the faculty buildings or quite possibly on the moons of Jupiter, the website didn't say.

Catherine was about to jump on her Vespa and find the board herself, when she remembered that prior to Kahn and Cerf inventing the internet there had been another nifty invention by one Alexander Graham Bell.

It took three full minutes to find any phone number at all for the university. After scrolling through three separate "contact us" web forms which would no doubt be seen by a human eventually, Catherine found a switchboard number and dialled it. After a five-minute wait for the receptionist to find the zoology department's number on the uni's own intranet, Catherine heard a languid, deep voice.

'Zoology.'

'Hello, I'm trying to find the lecturing schedule for Professor Simon Forster.'

'Hmm, you mean Associate Professor Forster.'

It occurred to Catherine that this human, whose name she didn't know, would regularly talk to people frustrated with the university's IT systems, students frustrated by work or staff trying to find the noticeboard. This man had created more cancer than cigarettes.

She pinched the bridge of her nose. 'Wait, let me check that, associate, associate,' she mimicked a person going through a diary. 'Oh, yes here it is. I don't care. When does he lecture?'

There was a pause; there was the sound of a well-fed throat clearing. 'You're a student at the faculty?'

'Yes.' Catherine answered with barely a moment's pause.

'Your name?'

'Boris Shakhovskoy.' She was glad she hadn't gone in.

'Student number?'

'8966112.' Which had been her number, she'd added a digit for the passing of time. If he looked it up she'd be caught out but she was betting on him being too lazy to do so.

She heard the clicking of a keyboard and held her breath.

It continued and her lungs started to hurt so she breathed as quietly and deeply as she could, her body and soul recuperating from the ravages of the Melbourne Uni IT system. Eventually the voice returned.

'Associate Professor Forster's lectures are on Mondays, Tuesdays and Thursdays eight and eleven in the ante meridian and four post meridian.'

'Thank you.'

'Is there anything else you require?'

'No, may the sun shine up your day.'

She had hung up before he could say, 'and up yours.'

She exhaled. People like that explain all wars, all genocide. You would avoid them if you could, but they're everywhere.

The attack had occurred on a Monday. At approximately 8.45am, according to Bradbury. Simon would have been well off the site at that time. As odd as he was, it appeared he was no killer.

After this, she spent time looking into the lives of Georgia Potter and Ian Bradbury.

Georgia had, her professional networking page told Catherine, graduated from a business and commerce degree some thirty years ago and moved straight into banking. Working with two out of the "big four" of Australian banks over the next two decades, she'd had a meteoric rise. Catherine didn't have a head for corporate speak but understood that the fancier your title, the more you were paid. Georgia's CV was a chart of increasing syllables in job titles, leaving you to think that if she hadn't moved to the zoo she could be the Senior Executive Performance Support Manager for the Department of Radiosacred Cash-Cows by now.

She had been on the zoo board for ten years, leaving her last banking job two years ago to become chairperson of the board and managing director of Zoos Victoria.

There was nothing listed about family. Though Catherine supposed there wouldn't be on such a site. She flicked to her own for comparison, and found that she was a brilliant young milliner who looked like she ran a much more successful business than her accountant told her. Nothing about friends, nothing about values, nothing about the mysteries she had solved. Such sites were like strange boring avatars, all success and no reality, casting us all as Superman with a flowing cape of beige.

Bradbury, of course, had his own website. It catalogued an impressive list of series, awards and initiatives from his work in bringing the southern quoll back from extinction to his five Emmy awards, four BAFTAs and a Logie, for nature documentaries. Catherine felt a moment of sheer inadequacy. The man had been brilliant since he was five-years-old.

Sometimes, a teacher once told her, we experience people who appear to have been born fully formed. They are the most impressive and dangerous of all people.

Catherine was just thinking that years on she didn't know what that meant, until her breath caught on a line in the bio.

Ian single-handedly rescued a fellow zoologist from an attack in a gorilla enclosure at the Los Angeles Zoo. Read about it *here*.

Catherine followed the link.

Forty minutes later she was still reading.

She broke for lunch. Guilt brought her to the hats again. She spent a fruitful hour on the green and even blocked up a bowler, obviously inspired by Bradbury's pretence at thinking about buying one of her works.

To end the one-way traffic, Catherine rang Philomena, who while not surprised by the contact – why would she be? – was glad for the update that Catherine's work would come to fruition by the agreed deadline of Wednesday.

The only unproductive parts of the day came as Catherine found herself subconsciously plotting on how she could sabotage the hat while keeping it beautiful. They came in quarter-hour blocks. She even looked up "migraine inspiring magnets" that could be sewn in, before she shook herself out of it.

The afternoon came and the clouds looked ominous. Catherine decided it wasn't necessary to be on the ground at the zoo in such weather. Which left at-home investigation, also known as phone work. Certain phone calls you don't want to make because they are going to be difficult, others because they are too easy. It took Catherine a minute of thinking about Beau to dial the number.

'Hello, Ms Marple. I'm delighted to hear from you.'

Catherine's eyes glazed. Some men were hard nuts to crack. Others were as challenging as a cruise buffet, making them about as appealing.

'Andy, how are you?'

'Fine. Burning the midnight oil here.'

Catherine nodded disinterestedly. 'If I said the words: Ian Bradbury, hero. What would you say?'

'I'd say, um, makes great documentaries.'

'Anything more exciting?'

'Oh, you mean what he did? Yeah that was out there. We're,' his voice grew quieter, 'well we've been told not to mention it. Comes from the top. Apparently he's quite shy about it.'

Catherine's eyebrow twitched. 'Hmm, interesting. So, tell me what you know?'

'About that? Just let me go for a walk.' She listened to the sounds of him leaving his desk and going outside. It was raining. This fella liked her, no question. He came back on the line. 'Apparently, he threw some meat to the dogs and pulled Beau out, pretty brave really.'

'And no one has told the papers?'

'Management is keeping a close eye on us, my boss is walking towards me right now.'

'Ask me out to dinner.'

'When?'

'It doesn't matter when, just ask me on a date right now.'

'I really like the roo at the Napier, would you like to meet me there on Thursday night?'

'That's good, is your boss still around?'

'No, she's turned around. So, Thursday?'

'No dear, that was just to get you off the hook.'

There were a few seconds of silence as he processed this. 'Right, I get it. Thanks.'

'My pleasure.' He wasn't so dumb, but not so smart either. Perhaps he was distracted by her beauty. Catherine looked at her nails and did an involuntary shimmy. 'Now, tell me what else you know.'

'That's about all. Bradbury made a call over the radio and people flocked to help. The ambulance was here in eight minutes.'

The rain was coming harder on her window. It would hit the zoo in a few minutes if the wind kept up. 'Okay, thanks Andy. I'll be in touch.'

'So, Thursday was a smokescreen?' He paused. 'Just to be sure.'

'Keen, aren't you?'

'Not many people bring intrigue and an appreciation of whistling into my life. It's hard not to be excited.'

Catherine closed her eyes. Somewhere Beau was still breathing; machines were working and Bradbury was full of it. 'There's a lot of Thursdays until the planet explodes, Andy. Patience is a virtue.'

'And amazing pub food is a gift.'

'On that we concur.' She hung up. It was 5.45. She wondered if Boris was at work.

'Glasgow Palace, this is Boris.'

Catherine blinked. 'I called your mobile.'

'Successfully. That's my way of telling you I'm at work.'

'Good. I'm coming up. I need help.'

'So do I, Jamie called in sick. Can you wash dishes?'

She looked at her sink. 'It's a funny thing, you know I've never tried.'

'I knew you'd say that. Want me to order you a salad?'

'No, in fact I'll have a porterhouse steak with extra chips covered in blood and a side order of Chicken Kiev, nuggets and a pint of mushroom gravy.'

He was quiet for a full three seconds, a long time when the bar is busy. 'You are evil.'

Catherine felt brighter. 'See you soon.'

The rain had paused, though as she walked on to Albion Street a cold wind blew through her. It was the kind of wind Melburnians hate because it speaks of sideways rain, bone chilling mornings, grey skies and more uncaring wind than is needed in your average Hemingway novel. A preview of yet another unwelcome winter. Catherine scrunched her eyes and viewed the variation in grey as the wet sky flickered in the last of the day's light. It was beautiful, cold and somehow more like space than earth.

Her phone rang. She ducked back into the alcove of her apartment door and took the call.

'This is Catherine.'

'Catherine Kint?'

'Yes, that's me.'

'This is Belinda Farrell in ICU at St Vincent's, I've been looking after Beau Hacska.'

Catherine's feet stopped before she told them to. She heard the voice, listened to the modulation and felt colder still. 'Has he, is he?'

'I'm sorry Catherine, his vitals are fading. Would you like to come in?'

She took the Vespa in. It was stupid to ride in the rain, especially when a new friend is about to become a memory. Yet she did, and was conscious of the rain against her visor the whole time. She was sure there had been traffic lights, but all she could think about were his hands.

Belinda was there, as was Georgia and a woman of about sixty. Georgia was holding her.

'Phyllis, this is Catherine.' Belinda's voice was professional. Not bright, not despairing, Catherine imagined these scenes were part of her daily working life.

Phyllis shook her hand and smiled. A strange silence overcome Catherine. Her brain was numb and she became driven by the urge to make it easier for this woman. 'He looks like you.'

Phyllis looked at him. 'He does, doesn't he?'

At that moment, his features were so warped by tubes he didn't resemble anyone much.

Five minutes later, he was gone.

Catherine stood for a long time next to his bed. Listening to his mother cry, aware of Georgia shaking, her whole body shaking. Belinda was in the background, preparing paperwork that Catherine was glad she would have no part in signing. She looked at Georgia, who made eye contact. Catherine knew she should say something, something human, yet nothing came. Until she knew Georgia wasn't behind it, she couldn't pretend she cared. Georgia tried to control herself, but couldn't, and just shook. Catherine saw her take a packet of cigarettes out of her bag. She walked out a second later.

'I've been in Europe,' said Phyllis, her voice hoarse, 'that's why I didn't come until today.'

Catherine took her hand and held her. 'I'm so sorry. I only knew him a few days.'

Phyllis didn't look away from her son. 'Was he happy?'

Catherine swallowed. 'He was. I think he really liked being alive.'

'He was nearly always so happy.'

She started crying again. Catherine held her, watching Beau's hand growing colder in his mother's grip.

An hour later she wandered towards the doors of the Glasgow Palace. She saw her own reflection in the glass doorway and for a moment felt red spite because she, a drunk and a fool, was alive and Beau, who saved animals, was cold.

No one called the universe fair. That didn't mean that it didn't deserve throttling.

Her reflection bowed and shifted as the door opened and she didn't even know it was Boris until she smelled his arms around her and his chest against her face. She sobbed once. Only once. Then he turned and she followed him inside.

Sometime later, Boris was touching on an earlier theme, and feeling more sober than he had in living memory. 'Remember Catherine, we're just stardust.' He put the drink in front of her.

Catherine took it. 'What we are, my dear, is dust. Dust that is getting sucked slowly or quickly into a black pit at the centre, or just off centre of the universe. It doesn't matter, because it is black and silent and we aren't even aware of it, so there is nothing to mourn. That happens to those left behind.'

Boris nodded, happy she hadn't noticed the tonic had no gin in it. 'I can't argue with this, except to say that Twisties are very tasty.'

Catherine drank. 'Yep.'

Either Boris was going up a wall or her head had hit the bar. 'We are just awake enough to enjoy distractions; some are meaningful and some aren't. It's all too hard some days. I should go to sleep.'

'It's good practice for the blackness, I'm told.'

'Aren't you supposed to be cheering me up?'

She looked around the bar and noticed that everyone else had left and the chairs were on the tables.

'Wouldn't that be an insult to your intelligence?'

She wobbled on her stool. 'Well, quite.'

'Let me take you home.'

Catherine was barely aware of anything aside from Boris' warmth. The night was cold. She heard someone singing badly, realised it was her. She leaned against a wall and saw Boris taking her keys out of her bag. The last thing she remembered was the cat jumping on her chest as Boris closed the door with a very soft bump.

8

Some are so great that even to stand near them is to be a god.

~ Simon Forster

There was pain, and a twin pressure. One on her abdomen, which was constant, potentially explosive. The other was a pounding, repetitive crashing against the inside of her eyes.

One was the phone, the other her guts. Catherine rolled off the couch and fell heavily.

Her phone, chiming, private number. Seven in the morning. Head like a concrete cake with an ice pick through it. Let guilt be your guide. Answer the phone Catherine, the bathroom will wait.

'This is Catherine.'

'You sound terrible.'

Female voice, good feeling, smart. 'Britt.'

'That's Detective Britt. We should talk.'

Catherine's chin rested on the glass of her coffee table. It felt cool, and a little dusty. 'I'm all ears.'

'I'm on the case.'

'Case?' Catherine's mouth tasted like a Martian ash field.

'Beau Hacska. It's now a suspected homicide.'

Pain in her guts as Beau's name was mentioned. The idea of revenge, and help, was welcome. 'Good.'

'So, the zoo in an hour?'

Catherine avoided putting her head horizontally on the table.

'Yep.'

'Are you all right?'

She stifled a yawn. 'Fine. I've been jogging.'

'An hour and a half then. Oh, I'm sorry for your loss.'

'You sound like Williams already.'

'Hmm, he doesn't need to know I'm talking to you.'

Catherine blearily made a pistol with the hand not holding the phone, only vaguely aware that Britt wouldn't be able to see it. 'Good plan.'

Over the next hour, Catherine groaned more than she usually did in a month. Hangovers are strange things. As a drinker of some experience Catherine had long ago decided that it was Russian roulette and occasionally you would cop it. Today was one of those days. She showered, ate hummus, eggs and toast and drank water and coffee in vast quantities. Now it was simply a matter of time and ignoring the voices that advised her to lie on the couch or be consumed with regret.

There were the memories though. Every drinker has them. Forgotten titbits of the past that you never think of until your brain decides it's vulnerable and says, 'Hey, remember this?'

For Catherine, it was the day the hair dye didn't work while on school camp, the bleach burning her scalp and the triumph in Grace's voice as she told the head mistress. The sound of laughter ringing through a dormitory and into the seared flesh of a fifteen-year-old's head.

That same head was hurting, years later, when the phone went again as she dragged herself to the shower. Philomena. There was no force on earth that would make Catherine answer that call. Grace had found a modern way to torment her.

Catherine banished the idea and turned on the tap, counting her blessings.

For one, she felt blessed not to be someone else, like someone with small children, or a job in drilling.

Philomena had sent a text: *I sense you are unwell, can I help?*

The situation was getting oppressive.

She didn't feel steady enough for the Vespa, and after doubling down on breakfast she needed time to shut her eyes. The train bobbed in an almost alive kind of way, more like a sadistic toddler than anything else. Her fellow passengers again made her feel like the only one truly awake as they stared into phones or out windows or, in one case, into nothing. She almost slept at one point, but stopped it. She thought of Beau until she was angry, not an emotion she usually encouraged in herself, but if anger was going to pull her through the hangover, then anger it was.

Somebody knew what happened; somebody hurt him. Somebody was going away for it. Even if Beau was beyond all concern, she owed it to his mother, Phyllis; and the next Beau.

At the zoo, she flashed her yearly pass and went inside. The day was grey and the crowds were daily getting smaller with the temperature cooling. Catherine blinked and drank in the atmosphere, finding it tepid. Then she took out her phone.

'Hey.' Britt was in work mode.

'I'm here.'

'Meet me at the African dogs. You know where they are, don't you?'

'Sure do.'

Twenty seconds later she saw Britt coming past the long grass. Catherine couldn't help but smile. In a dark pantsuit, Britt looked every inch a detective. Catherine swore she looked taller. She checked for heels.

Britt smiled at her, cradling a clipboard. A pen behind her ear pushed her blonde hair back. She was with a few other uniforms and plain-clothes, though clearly in charge.

'Hey.'

Neither of them moved to embrace. This was business. Catherine spoke quietly so no one could hear. 'Congratulations, Detective.'

'Thanks.' Britt mimicked her volume, then turned it up. 'So what have you found thus far?'

Catherine blinked and reported. 'The attack occurred on Monday last about 8.45 in the morning. There are no known witnesses aside from Ian Bradbury. Ian states that he heard a commotion and found Beau Hacska was being attacked by five dogs. Ian distracted the dogs by throwing meat to the far end of the enclosure and he pulled Beau out. I noted the substantial amount of blood lost by the victim,' she grimaced as she said this, 'and also the defence wounds on his hands. The attack was sustained and vigorously defended against.'

Britt took notes. 'You don't subscribe to the self-harm theory offered by certain zoo staff members?'

'Speaking as an acquaintance of the victim, the theory doesn't stand up.'

'Have you examined the doors and locks?'

Catherine smiled. 'As a civilian I had no access to view these.'

Britt's eyebrows raised almost imperceptibly. 'Never stopped you before.' Louder, she said, 'Come and have a look.'

'The blue set of keys,' Catherine murmured to no one in particular.

They moved briskly, Catherine feeling the familiar urgency of police work, ignoring how comfortable it felt. Britt didn't look at her as she spoke with her eyes focused on what was before her. 'I've authorised the funeral for tomorrow.'

'Tomorrow?' Catherine missed a step. 'No autopsy?'

Britt looked back, only for a second.

'We already know everything about what actually killed him: infection, caused by the wounds. A genome particular to the dogs was found in his bloodstream. We have the bloods and the full medical reports, what we don't know is the circumstances. Hence, we're here.'

'Tomorrow seems very quick.'

'It's his mother's wish. She has to get back to Europe.' Britt expression softened. 'Come look over here.'

Britt pulled her towards the side of the path, mimicked pointing a finger, and whispered, 'Hey, I'm not a cop for a second. Are you all right?'

'I'm fine. Thanks.'

Usual volume again. 'Come through here.' She led Catherine into the no access zone.

She ducked towards a far and previously concealed door in the enclosure, swiping a visitor's pass on an electric scanner.

The door led to a simple alcove, with a window to view the dogs inside. A bald, bespectacled man wearing zoo-keeper greens met them. He held out a hand to Catherine. 'Peter Cartledge, I'm a keeper here.'

Britt's eyes were on the dogs. 'Peter is our zoo liaison. He also has the keys and knows a fair bit about these animals.'

Catherine shook her head at the dogs' smiling canine faces, then turned back to the task at hand. Beside them was a simple penning area. Britt indicated it – 'That's where the dogs should have been waiting while Beau was working in their enclosure. I've gone over records and it was scheduled routine maintenance. I find it odd that it was authorised and crossed checked only by one person – Beau.'

Catherine's head throbbed. 'That does seem odd.' Catherine would have thought he would have been crossing his t's with the heat of Dong Zei's death on him.

Peter piped up, 'It does happen on occasion, especially early in the morning, if you notice something that needs doing and no one else is around.'

Britt nodded, her hand swept the penned-off area. 'So, the keeper would generally have used this door to access the enclosure and the dogs that far door?'

She indicated a smaller portal at the far end of the penning area. Peter nodded.

'Do you have a theory on which door was opened for the dogs to come out?'

Britt shook her head. 'Not a fool-proof one, though the animal door seems most likely.' She pointed. 'For them to have used the human door they would have had to get out of the penning area as well.'

'Could they jump?'

'I've been told yes.'

She looked to Peter, who again nodded. 'It's rare, but it is possible.'

'That could explain why only some of the dogs escaped. There were seventeen African wild dogs, now sixteen, with one in the infirmary. Only five were involved in the attack. The issue is that if that were the case and another human opened the door, why didn't the dogs attack that human?'

'Spoken to their keeper?'

'I'll be doing that, have no doubt.'

'What's his name?'

'There's three, though one was on leave.'

'And another,' Britt grimaced, 'is no longer alive. The third keeper's name is Simon Forster.'

Catherine kept her face blank, unsure of Peter's allegiance. 'I'd like to know how that interview goes.'

Britt nodded. 'As protocol allows.'

Catherine gave a slow wink, 'I understand.'

Britt took her over to the far end, ostensibly to point something out. She whispered, 'You've spoken with him?'

'Forster? I have. He has an alibi. He lectures at the local university at that time.'

'I'll look into it.'

'Good luck on the IT system.'

Britt raised an eyebrow. As they spoke they had approached the animal door. Britt had a set of keys.

Catherine put a hand on Britt's shoulder as she moved to unlock the door. 'Detective, isn't that a little gung ho?'

Britt indicated to Peter, who was standing with a tranquiliser gun. She pursed her lips and called over her shoulder, 'Dunstan.'

'Yep?' replied a waiting uniform.

'Draw your weapon, just in case.' She looked pointedly at Catherine. 'Okay?'

Catherine looked to Peter, who was now sweating. She moved back slightly as Britt turned the key and pushed the door open a centimetre and brought it back. She turned to Catherine. 'That one works.'

They moved back past the penning area. Catherine could hear a scratching against the recently opened animal door. Britt tried the second door, nodding at Dunstan who held his gun far too lovingly for Catherine's liking. That key also fitted and the latch turned smoothly.

Catherine looked around the room. The chamber was about four metres by five. There was access to running water and an electrical socket a metre and a half from the ground. The ceiling was about two and a half metres, a small window at the topmost part, though most light came from the floor-to-ceiling window on the enclosure side. Above both doors used by zoo-keepers were steel light fittings for tube fluorescents. The fitting was bent above the animal door. There was a wide trough for the animals in the penning area and a raised area of dried dirt.

There was no sign of blood. Both keyholes on further inspection showed no indication of forced entry or tampering. It had been four days. There were more unknowns than knowns.

The door from the main zoo opened. Catherine saw Britt stiffen slightly. In walked a man in a grey suit. His hair was more silver than a year ago, though his face was just as alert. It was the kind of face you could strike a match off, something Catherine had thought of several times in the years they had worked together, long ago. For a second Catherine thought he would smile, but he was impassive. His eyes moved from her and then to Britt as he gave a curt nod.

'Hello, sir.' Britt's shoulders fell back. Catherine nudged her.

'Hello, Ken.'

Detective Sergeant Kenneth Williams smiled ever so briefly. 'Good to see you, Catherine. Didn't know you liked animals.'

'My horizons are pretty broad.'

'You look tired. Rough night?'

Catherine's stomach did a turn. Hungover was fine, hungover in front of Williams was appalling. 'Lost a friend.'

'Sorry. Detective Houden, with me please?'

Catherine heard the breezy tone, and was ninety per cent sure she knew exactly what it meant. She scanned the area again, committing it to memory.

With Britt out of the way she turned to Peter. 'I'm sorry for your loss. Did you know Beau well?'

'I've worked with him most days for the past six months. A good man.'

'Tell me, is it regular for dogs to attack?'

'It's rare. Especially to attack a person they knew. That's what's got me. I've worked with these dogs for the past four years and I've never known them to do anything like this.'

'Were you in Melbourne while on leave?'

He shook his head, hands in pockets. 'No, I flew in from Borneo yesterday.'

'Working with animals?'

'I was on holiday; trying to observe clouded leopards.' He smiled, as if he understood and enjoyed that he was a cliché.

She couldn't help but smile. 'You love animals.'

'We all do.' He turned sadly to the window. 'You just can't predict them all the time.'

Catherine put a hand to his shoulder. 'Then there's humans.'

He smiled. She thought he got the joke.

Catherine had spent fifteen more minutes in the alcove. She re-examined both doors and then looked over every aspect she could, moving in a wider circuit each time as her training had taught her, asking lots of questions. She noticed a crack in the top right corner of the window, but Peter said it had been damaged some two years ago.

There had been a good deal of traffic through the area since the crime: police, medics, zoo staff and people in her old profession – crime scene investigators. She could see remnants of the fingerprint powders.

Footprints would have been long gone. Hair, skin, impossible to find and verify without resources she no longer had access to.

Britt walked back in. Didn't look at Catherine. 'Peter, could you take me through the maintenance logs again. I want to know more about the log-ons and passwords.'

'Fine detective, no problem.'

They moved out. Britt caught Catherine's gaze momentarily. Catherine had no idea what the look was supposed to mean.

'Ms Kint.' She turned to find the uniform that Britt had called Dunstan. He was young to be so bald.

'Yes.'

'This is a crime scene. I'm going to have to ask you to step outside now.'

He gave a little smile, knowing it was a dance.

'Detective Houden asked me here.'

'It's time to go.' He was far too relaxed to ever be a detective. She followed the direction of his arm to the door.

If she hadn't had two coffees before she left the zoo, she would have fallen asleep on the train. As it was she was thinking about a nap when she opened her front door. Only to find Philomena ringing her again.

Catherine ignored it and moved into the bedroom. She was never one for sleeping during the day, but there was a certain justification when murder, hangovers, betrayal and Williams all converge. It's probably in the Magna Carta.

As her head hit the pillow she saw something behind her bedside drawers. Some green material was jammed between the wall and the back of the drawers. Catherine reached for it and was amazed to find tears in her eyes.

It was a thick khaki sock. Beau's sock.

She gripped it tightly and sighed. There was even something viscous and green smeared on one side. She fell asleep holding it.

Hours later, her hangover and her anger had vanished. Her anger was an extra layer of feeling lining her entire nervous system, and easy to ignore unless provoked.

When she rang, Boris picked up quickly. 'I'm not at work.'

Catherine's eyes narrowed. 'No, you're not. And you are nervous. Is it date night tonight?'

'Yes, and what do you mean I'm nervous? I'm terrified.'

Catherine sighed. 'Why?' Even she thought she sounded impatient.

'Because I'm terrible at this. Have we met?'

'Yes, on several plains of consciousness and in all of them you have shown valour and good humour. So, it amazes me how you play into overdramatising romance so often.'

Boris sounded dejected. 'You love romance.'

'I do, but you've swallowed this "hopeless in love" bizzo hook, line and sinker. It's bad for your posture.' She smirked as she imagined him straightening up.

'Why are you ringing?'

'I want help on the case. New facts are coming to light.'

'You want me to cancel?'

'You know I don't, but thanks for offering. I need you in full control of your faculties. Come by afterwards.'

He snorted. 'See you in forty-five minutes then.'

'Don't be a twerp.'

'Okay, I may see you. I could be busy tonight, all night.'

'Now you're talking, see you before midnight then.'

He hung up the phone. He wasn't going to get nervous. Not until she was fifteen minutes late. The small beach ball in his stomach was surely more to do with the cheese on toast he had eaten an hour earlier. He kept looking at the clock. Waiting, not so much for when Molly said she would come, but when he could worry about her being late. It wasn't a strategy he had ever articulated to anyone, or even come up with deliberately. It was just a motion he went through.

Like many single people who didn't want to be, he had spent the day thinking hard about the single experience. Or, to put it another way, what had gone wrong the last five times he had gone out with a girl.

He tried too hard.

She didn't think he was funny.

She "wasn't racist, but hated the Lebanese".

She hated Catherine without meeting her.

He tried too hard.

The racism aside, it was a case of not finding the right person. Or, possibly, of being completely worthless and unlovable as a human being.

Catherine had always said it would happen and happen quickly when a woman realised everything that was great about him. He had never mentioned it because it would seem churlish, that she nearly always said that with some tall dark and handsome fellow on her arm. Some of those men were indeed "great", but their greatness seemed easier to notice because of the high cheek bones and strong pectorals that were *de rigueur* with her lovers.

He had checked his outfit, hair and smile for the zillionth time and was thinking about a beer to loosen up when his phone vibrated and chimed loudly – he had the volume up to full so he wouldn't miss her text. He picked up the phone and saw Molly: *Out front. X.*

X, there was an X already, and she was early. This felt strange, almost like it wasn't a disaster. Or did it mean she was an axe murderer? Or worse, another racist? Boris didn't regret his rant about loving Brunswick and multiculturalism equally on that fateful night, but he deeply regretted listening to his date talking about "those people" for twenty minutes before he piped up.

He shook his head. Molly seemed confident and fun. She was vegetarian and aside from seeming to like him, had no other indications of psychological flaws.

He opened the door. 'Hi.'

'Hi.' She put her phone into her back pocket. She smiled at him. 'You didn't wear the t-shirt?'

'Spock?'

'Yeah, I thought it would be cute.'

'I almost did, but didn't want to be cute.'

She kissed him on the cheek, kept a hand on his shoulder. 'You are cute, so be it. Can I come in while you change?'

He was dreaming, surely. 'Want a beer?'

'Love one.'

Boris couldn't stop grinning as he climbed the stairs. Best. Day. Ever.

Two hours later, Boris found himself enjoying vegetarian food in a way he never had in all the previous years of his life. The restaurant was bustling, if not crowded. He and Molly enjoyed a booth to themselves. Two empty beer jugs were hidden at the wall end of the table with a fresh one between their two plates. The lighting of the restaurant made Boris' now pink t-shirt seem a deep red.

'This is great! What do you call this again?'

'That, my fine friend, is grilled tempeh, marinated in chilli and soy sauce. It's not horrible for you and is full of the protein you once got from chicken parmigiana.'

'It's good. I'd prefer a parma, if I'm completely honest, but I like it.'

She grinned and passed him a napkin. 'You didn't call me about the soy milk thing.'

Boris looked up sharply, from wiping his beard. 'I didn't, damn.'

'That's okay. What I was going to tell you was basically this: you have soy milk, say a soy coffee, and it's different to what you've had in the past. You can either hate it because it's different to previous experience, or judge it on its merits. I had to switch to soy milk a few years ago – it became my all-pervasive theory on life.'

'So, me not comparing this to a parma?'

'Means you enjoy the tempeh, or don't enjoy it, on its merits.'

'Cool theory.' Boris saluted with his fork. 'I'm sure it's in Buddhist somewhere.'

'Probably.' Molly leaned forward. 'What have you been eating?'

'Stir frys, lots of cheese on toast.'

She smiled. 'I can help you with this. Are any of your friends vego?'

Boris looked towards the ceiling as he thought about it. 'Not that I can think of.'

'What made you change? Usually it's a contagious thing, vego thoughts beget vegos.'

Boris took a sip and then spoke. 'I was thinking about racism, sexism and homophobia. What my grandfather thought was acceptable and what I think is acceptable are very different things. That led to the thought of what my grandchildren would think, and what they would find antiquated about my attitudes. I guess I figured the next thing to fix was unnecessary animal deaths.' He patted his stomach, 'I'm well fed and have been for a long time. It seemed like the right thing.'

'You're a treat, Boris.'

Boris smiled into his tempeh. 'How long have you been vegetarian?'

'Sixteen years. When my Dad showed me one of the lambs he was about to slaughter. He showed my brother and me, wanting us to know what happened. I wanted no part in it afterwards.'

'What about your brother?'

'He understood, too. He was just more comfortable with the world than I was. Still is. Hence, he eats meat.'

Boris wondered briefly which approach was more logical and if Vulcans ate meat. He refocused on Molly. 'Was your Dad mad?'

'No, I think he knew it might play out that way. For a farmer he was pretty good like that. Mum was furious for a long time, but more at him than at me. Especially as she had to cook extra meals afterwards. She got over it.'

'How did you go living on a farm that made meat without eating it?'

'The same as you go living in a world of chicken parmas without eating one.'

Boris put down his chopsticks. 'It's day four.'

'Only for a little while. Do you want another?' She gestured to his beer and reached for the empty jug.

'Please.'

While she went to the bar, his pocket vibrated. Catherine.

'Make it quick, I'm on a date.'

'I know, but if you don't sleep with her I still need help, and also tonic, can you bring some?'

'Yes.' He rolled his eyes, 'Unless...'

'Don't jinx yourself, dear.'

'I didn't want to; I have to go.'

'Good luck, captain.'

As he put the phone down Molly returned. An eyebrow told him he had been sprung.

'Thanks, that was my friend Catherine.'

'"My friend" Catherine?'

'Yes,' he said, pouring beer and trying to think diplomatically. 'Some people can't believe we're friends. So I, um...'

Molly was fixing him with a look he hadn't seen on her. It would have wilted the lettuce if she had turned it on the salad.

'So I use, "my friend" as, like a prefix so you, and people don't...'

Molly suddenly laughed, snorting.

Boris, horrified, dropped his chopsticks and reached to pat her on the back. She waved him away.

'I'm sorry,' she snorted again, and then started laughing harder. Boris, suddenly feeling like all might not be lost, began to smile too.

In a minute Molly's laughter paused. 'You just looked so profoundly uncomfortable, I couldn't resist.'

Boris exhaled and took a long drink of beer. For some reason, he found Molly teasing him so effectively very endearing, if somewhat familiar.

Molly had composed herself, though was still grinning. 'So you have a friend called Catherine, and it's bitten you before. So you call her 'My Friend' right?'

Boris nodded.

'Is she pretty?'

Boris shrugged an affirmative.

'Is she smart?'

'Yes.'

'What are her boobs like?'

Boris almost spat beer. 'What?'

Molly grinned. 'Is she your ex?'

'No, not at all. It's just we're close. And yes, once I went out with a girl for a few weeks and she couldn't deal with me having a friend who was a girl, too. So, I know it's dumb, but...'

'Boris, we're having dinner. Do you really think it's any of my business?'

'Well, we're having dinner.'

Molly smiled again. The lights of the restaurant made her the most wonderful thing he had ever seen. 'That's the right answer. You're doing all right in life.'

Around midnight, there was a knock on Catherine's door. Boris was beaming. He put down the tonic and hugged her tenderly. 'You okay?'

'For once, my dear, no I'm not. Don't let that spoil your mood though. Is the sky purple?'

'It is, the air is fresh and I got a smooch from a pretty girl. I think I may have a girlfriend.'

'Has she indicated such a meeting of souls?'

'No, nor have we gone any further than a pash on Lygon Street, but I like to dream big.'

Catherine clapped him on the shoulder. 'Never stop doing that.'

Boris helped himself to a beer from the fridge and looked towards her drink, instinctively making her a gin with the fresh tonic. They visited the balcony before, shivering, they both retreated to the lounge room.

'Autumn is a real harbinger some days, isn't it?'

'Oh God Boris, a harbinger? You are in a good mood. A week ago you just said, "shit it's cold".'

He sat. 'I think I've had a much better day than you. I'm sorry, I meant to call this morning.'

Catherine waved him away. 'Thanks for looking after me, I was obviously a mess.' She sat down in her usual position. 'I forgot parts and felt dreadful all day.'

'What did you do?'

'Britt's on Beau's case. I helped, I saw the doors that were opened to kill him. Williams turned up and I got turfed out.'

Boris nodded at her glass. 'How many of those have you had?'

'Not enough.'

'Let's talk.'

They quickly took their usual positions around the coffee table. Catherine began. 'So, first let's assume that someone killed Beau deliberately. Let's look at motive. Who's got one?'

'The whole planet because he was with you and they weren't?'

Catherine looked perplexed. 'Why would you say that?'

'You've had a bad day champ, you needed geeing up.'

She sipped her drink. 'Aside from my allure, who's got Beau in their sights?'

'He sounded like a thorn in management's side over the elephant. So let's blame management.'

'Leon would love how quickly you came to that conclusion.'

Boris' eyes widened. 'He's threatened to kill me twice this year.'

'Which shows he has the patience of a saint.'

Boris snorted. Catherine continued unabashed. 'All right, so let's look at Georgia. She has something to gain from him not being around, but was nowhere near the enclosure on the day.'

'How do you know that?'

'To be honest I don't, but I have to have some faith in the police, or at the very least in Britt to have checked.'

'Check again. You said she was at the hospital most days.'

'Yes, and she was there when he died.'

'Did she look happy?'

'Quite the opposite.'

'There you go.' He took a triumphant swing of beer.

'There you go, what? She's unhappy because she realises that she killed someone in the heat of the moment, or she's unhappy because someone has died, or she is happy but manages to conceal it.'

Boris finished his beer. 'I take your point, but there's a silver lining.'

'What?'

'We have more time to ponder this. Double?'

Catherine groaned. 'Why not, your good mood is irritating.' She rubbed her forehead while Boris rose to get more refreshments. 'She certainly seemed troubled, and I kept thinking of that Dylan line about standing over someone's grave to make sure that they're dead.'

'Was Bradbury ever at the hospital?'

'I didn't see him there.'

'What about other staff?'

'There were a few, and they sent flowers. Andy said they were told not to make a fuss, so perhaps they were kept in the dark?'

Boris leaned in, elbows on his knees. 'How do you not make a fuss about someone being attacked by wild dogs?'

'With extreme bullying and an iron fist.'

Boris sighed. 'Okay, moving on. Who else? Bradbury? What does he gain?'

Catherine fingered her glass. 'Well, he has a theory about the elephant dying from a virus, which Beau vigorously disputed.'

'Yeah, but he's Ian Bradbury, even if he was wrong most people would side with him.'

'Because he's on television?'

'Yeah.'

Catherine looked accusingly at her own screen. 'It's the royalty of the modern age, anyone on television has the same infallibility that the pope or a king had centuries ago.'

She leaned further in. 'Now here's the juicy part, Bradbury told me about saving Beau from the dogs. It was one of the bravest stories I'd heard in some time. Yet there was nothing about it in the papers.'

Boris sniffed, incredulous. 'And no one at the zoo is allowed to talk about it?'

'Right, now look at this from his website.' She turned her laptop around. Boris put down his beer and began reading.

'Goodness me,' said Boris.

Catherine smiled triumphantly. 'Yep, so twenty years ago, Bradbury saves a keeper from an aggravated gorilla in the States and then basically goes on a book tour about it. Last week he does something remarkably similar and suppresses the whole story?'

Boris scratched his head. 'Modesty?'

Catherine shook hers. 'Not when compared to his complete lack of modesty two decades ago.'

Boris closed the laptop. 'Perhaps that's the wisdom of being almost seventy.'

'Perhaps. I suspect there may be something more to it. I intend to ask the question when I see him next.'

'And when is that?'

'Tomorrow. Provided Williams hasn't barred me from the zoo.'

They sat in silence for a while. Catherine pondered what possible motivations Bradbury could have to hurt Beau while Boris thought eagerly of Molly and guiltily of eating a kebab. At this carnivorous thought, he looked up. 'What about the other bloke?'

'Which one?'

'The one, um,' he considered how many beers he had had since Molly had come over, 'the one who went off when the elephant died?'

'Oh, Simon. Well, he's Bradbury's right-hand man. They have a very strange relationship. Simon seems quite protective. He was annoyed when I was alone with Ian.'

'Lovers?'

Catherine made a face. 'I think Simon's an odd man who is best friends with a legend. He has an alibi – he was lecturing at Melbourne uni.'

Boris arched his back in a satisfied kind of way. 'Ah, uni lectures. I reckon I would have believed at least seventy per cent of the lecturers I had were capable of violent crime.'

'He's fit enough too. Part of my hesitation with suspecting Bradbury is anyone who was going to open the door to hurt Beau would have had to get out of the way of the dogs themselves.'

'Wouldn't Bradbury have a few tricks up his sleeve to distract the dogs while he put them on Beau's scent? I mean, if he's to be believed then he was able to move them quickly away from Beau when he rescued him.'

'I still can't quite see it. He's a sleaze. But at the same time a sweet old man, really.'

Boris snorted. 'And brave too.'

Catherine drained her glass. 'And he's been on television. Okay, knock off. I have to make an early morning phone call. See if Britt still wants to play with me.'

Boris stood and stretched, taking the empties to Catherine's kitchen before letting himself out. Catherine noticed that he seemed taller.

9

The pro-zoo argument gets even more depressing when you factor in which species we're protecting these animals from...

~ Beau Hacska

Catherine was on her second coffee when she made the call. It was seven in the morning but Britt sounded like she'd been up for hours.

Catherine shivered on the balcony. She was rugged up, but it was still cold. 'Can you talk?'

Britt sounded like she was working. Catherine could hear her typing as she spoke. 'Right now I can. Later, not so much.'

'Williams not happy?'

'I tried to push that you had insights, he countered how often they were wrong. Then there's the issue of blue.'

'Blue?'

'You don't wear it.'

'Christ.' Catherine shook her head. It shouldn't matter what he thought, but it did. 'I would take that, except he's always wearing grey.'

'What's your thoughts?'

'More questions than answers. Where was Potter when the accident happened? When does the elephant's case get closed? Why does Ian Bradbury not take a lap of honour when he saves someone?'

'He told me he's shy about that stuff.'

Catherine leaned over the railing. It was lovely to see the sky change colour. Her coffee mug spilled steam into the atmosphere. 'Did you see his interviews twenty years ago when a similar thing happened?'

'I did actually. Good pick up.'

'What did he say to that?'

'He said that he's a changed man in that regard, no longer thirsty for the limelight, also that Beau was in hospital made him quiet. I thought it held water.' She sounded tired. 'Catherine, I know you aren't going to like it but I'm leaning towards the self-harm theory. Hacska screws up, is about to be fired, and hurts himself either deliberately or by accident. Or even a self-immolation thing that hurts the zoo.'

'Bull.'

'I know it's personal.'

'Yes it is,' she said, too quickly with too much feeling. 'But I know I'm right. He just didn't.'

'Okay,' said Britt, also too quickly.

'What about Potter, does she have an alibi?'

'Potter,' Catherine could hear Britt flipping a page, imagined her at a desk. 'Potter, yep, solid alibi, she–'

Catherine heard a male voice say Britt's name.

'I have to go.'

The line went dead. Catherine was concerned until she realised Britt was in a police station, and she knew that voice.

She looked at the clock – 7.30, the time Williams started work. Oh dear.

There was no time to waste, she decided. Twenty-two minutes later Catherine had parked the Vespa and was out the front of Ian Bradbury's home. The clouds swirled against a cold blue sky and she shivered in her cadmium jacket. She had swapped her motorbike helmet for a classic black beret. Just before eight o'clock he emerged from the house, saw her and froze.

'Hi Ian, could I ask you a question?'

He walked slowly down the path. 'I'm not sure.'

'I'm sorry to ambush you.'

He looked away from her, clearing his throat. 'I liked it more when you popped round for tea.'

'I could come back later?'

'No,' he smiled apologetically, but his tone was firm. 'A definite no, I'm afraid.'

'I'll ask now then. Why keep your bravery so quiet when you saved Beau? You were happy to talk twenty years ago when you saved a keeper from a gorilla.'

Ian kept moving towards his car. 'Rachel, that was a very different situation. The keeper was safe. Beau died.'

'It's Catherine. It still seems strange that zoo staff were asked not to talk about it. Did that come from you?'

'Catherine.' He blinked apologetically. 'I didn't know that staff weren't allowed to discuss it. I thought this was Australia.'

'You're quite right there.'

'Although, I do believe there are certain conventions followed, when someone tries to take their own life.' He was at his car door now. 'I have to go now. Please don't be here when I get back.'

'You know that didn't happen. You said as much the other day.'

'I'm simply repeating.' He got into the car, started the motor and then wound a window down. 'Catherine, it's not a conspiracy against Beau, more of one for him.'

As he drove away Catherine felt a sting at the back of her head. Different to a gin hangover, this was a pin-prick that threatened to get bigger. She moved over to the fence and sat, holding her neck. Fighting away panic, she breathed as deeply as she could for the next three minutes. The pain began subsiding.

She'd been at the zoo for fifteen minutes. There was no sign of Georgia Potter, who was not taking calls. Catherine marched across the north court, phone to her ear as she left another message. Andy also hadn't taken a call, though she suspected that was more to do with the hour than avoiding her. To round out the three, Detective Britt Houden wasn't answering either. Catherine grimaced and decided it was a sign that many obstacles must be faced alone.

Out of the corner of her eye she saw a group of four people walking faster than the visitors. One of them in a navy pantsuit.

Catherine ran over; Britt walked faster.

'Britt.'

'I can't talk, Catherine.'

'Oh, come on.'

'Leave it, Catherine.'

The other three had stopped. One was Peter, the zoo liaison from the day before, the other two were cops. Dunstan from yesterday was in uniform and the other wore it in his walk.

'I don't leave things, Britt.'

Britt turned slowly. The others decelerated and then stopped. Catherine wondered if they were friends of Williams, here to watch Britt and make sure she kept her distance. Catherine didn't care. 'You're being sold a line on the suicide aspect. It might be a clean report, but it's not true.'

'I told you to walk, Catherine. I don't want to hear it.'

'Stop channelling Williams, you know I'm right.'

'I have access to more files than you, and I know that if you don't stop harassing staff I will have you arrested.'

Catherine reeled back. 'What?'

'Waiting outside people's houses might seem cute in your head but it's not how civilians behave. You're a civilian.' She spat the word. 'Remember that. You made a choice.'

Catherine didn't budge. 'I said stop channelling Williams. He won't be impressed.'

'Nor will Bradbury hesitate to put a restraining order on you if he so much as smells you near his house again. He's not a suspect. You're not a cop.' Her face was like stone, her anger real. She added a last barb. 'You have ten minutes to leave this premises. Dunstan, see Ms Kint follows that order, or take her to St Kilda Road.'

Britt turned away.

The headache was back, harder than before. Catherine watched her former friend walk away. Dunstan hung back, smiling his apologetic smile.

'Come on,' he said.

Catherine glared at him. 'You're doing it all wrong. You're supposed to be more commanding.'

He continued smiling. 'Yeah, I get that a lot. Yet no one actually resists. There's a time and a place for all that big dog stuff. Let's go.'

'No, I'm a member. You don't have jurisdiction.'

He looked away towards the exit and held a hand towards it. 'You might be a member but you're not here for your love of the red panda. Let's go.'

Catherine reluctantly started walking. 'You've seen the facts on this, you know it's bull–' Catherine had to stop talking and doubled over as the headache came with renewed intensity. For a moment she couldn't think of anything aside from the colour blue, pounding against her lower neck.

'Are you okay?'

Catherine breathed again. It receded. 'I'm fine.'

Dunstan stood close, but didn't touch her. 'No, by the way.'

'No what?'

'I don't think the suicide theory is crap. Also, we shouldn't take someone's emotionally compromised views as evidence.' He gestured again towards the exit. 'You're also not allowed to stalk people. You'd have got that in your training. Shall we?'

'You're the font of blue line wisdom, aren't you?'

'I'm popular.'

Catherine's voice was low. 'You know this won't stop me.'

She swallowed, instantly regretting it. Noticing Dunstan's whole air changed, and suddenly he looked quite like a cop indeed.

They walked slowly, Dunstan not pushing it, Catherine with as much dignity as possible. As they passed the seal enclosure she saw Simon walking towards them. He stopped, giving her a half smile. Catherine ignored it.

Bad day. It was time to think and make a hat, or at least attempt both.

The train was quiet, and soothing. That said, Catherine was so worked up that it could have been a movable day spa with hot and cold running gin taps and she would still be ready for murder. The world, even her friends, may think Beau wanted to hurt himself, but her gut told her otherwise. She tried to calm down. Then she remembered the funeral. For a minute she let herself imagine Beau sitting beside her.

She tried to focus on him, his memory, trying to think of anything aside from a dear friend threatening to have her arrested. Anything aside from Simon's smirk as she was escorted away. Anything aside from the words "you made a choice" and the cop club she had spurned that would never forgive her for it.

There was a newspaper on the seat as she got on, discarded in the morning rush. Catherine flicked through it. To cap off her morning, she found a puff piece about the Right Honourable Grace Chichester who injected billions into Victoria through her savvy cultivation of developers from around the world. The photo showed her smiling at a bunch of old men in suits more expensive than an average car. Catherine thought of a small explosive she could put in Philomena's hat.

Her phone rang. Andy.

'Tell me something good?'

'I'm tall, dark and handsome?'

She slapped the paper down next to her. 'Yep, sure you are, just keep telling yourself, girls love that.'

'Oh really, because I…'

'Don't make it worse. I have a question. Is the line about not discussing Beau's demise because it's a suspected suicide?'

'There's been nothing said officially, but it's a heavy undercurrent.'

Catherine leaned her head against the glass window of the train. 'Right.'

'I'm sorry for your loss, by the way.'

Her breath fogged the window. 'Thanks, but I barely knew him.'

'Well enough, I reckon.'

'Yep, well enough.'

He cleared his throat. 'You don't think it was suicide?'

'I'm pretty damn sure about it.'

'Want me to meet you? I'm at work now.'

Catherine stood as the train left Brunswick Station on the way to Anstey. 'I've been escorted from the place. I was asking too many questions.'

There was a silence. 'That's heavy. Who do you need to speak with?'

'I need answers from a few people. Ian Bradbury is on top of the list. Can you go and tie him up, please?'

Andy chuckled. 'No. I don't have a direct line. He's not on the staffing list. I can tell you that he's been working quite late recently. I could get the lab number for you? That's where he is mostly.'

'I'll take it, but I don't think he'll speak with me over the phone.'

'You could pretend to be a dead meerkat and surprise him when he goes to dissect you?'

'You know, you're in too good a mood for human consumption right now. I'm going.'

'So I'm told, see you later.'

She was almost home when the phone rang again. Catherine thought she might torch the damn thing. Private number.

'This is Catherine.'

'Williams.'

Some people who have spent a lifetime in various degrees of authority can use their own name as if it's a trump card. Williams did this. Catherine used to think herself impervious, but noticed today she straightened up as soon as he said it.

'What?'

'What, sir.'

Catherine took her keys out. 'All I've been told today is that I made a choice and so I can't be near the zoo. I'm not a cop, so you're not sir. What do you want, Ken?'

'I want you to know that if you don't butt out she'll fail.'

'She's already failing.' Diplomacy and loyalty were always secondary to the truth with Williams.

'Your presence will make it definite.'

Minty moved quickly out of her way as she put her bag on the bench. Catherine must have been sending out angry vibrations. 'I'm right on this. Are you pushing the suicide?'

'I'm pushing for a clean case. I've read the report, I make judgements with my head, unlike some.'

Catherine gripped the kitchen bench. 'You're wrong.'

'Good thing I'm not on the case, then. She is. Hear that? She is. Not you.'

'She's already told me that, why are you calling?'

'Some people need to be told repeatedly.'

'Not me.'

'I'm glad to hear it. Now behave yourself this afternoon.'

Catherine baulked at that. 'Jesus, Williams, don't tell me how to act at a funeral.'

He grunted. 'I shouldn't have to.'

'I think there's something wrong here.'

'And I think I'm going to get a result.'

Catherine was almost shouting, 'I think the truth is more important.'

'There's lots of truths, Catherine,' he replied quietly.

'I'm busy, that's one of them.'

'Don't need to tell me.' The phone went dead. Catherine found herself looking at the open wine bottle in the fridge. It was twenty minutes past ten.

Green felt, wave structure. It felt better in her hands than unanswered questions. Hats were hard to make but easy to understand. They worked or they didn't. Lives, and the end of lives, were not so simple. This made the end of lives harder to explain, because death and life represented a binary idea.

If the death meant nothing, life meant nothing. If the death could be lied about, then why have the life? If a death had been lied about, why on earth was she still making hats?

How could they be so content to write it off as self-harm? Beau's file must read like a horror film. If so, how had he seemed so stable when she had known him? He had been so sure of himself, interested in the world, plus his job had given him meaning. She cut and almost tore the fabric, swore under her breath, then thought of Beau. He wouldn't have been put in a tailspin by small mistakes.

Little mistakes were easily worked though.

Little mistakes. Like calling someone the wrong name.

Like talking to someone when you shouldn't.

Bradbury had called her Rachel. Was that his granddaughter's name? Catherine thought back to his mantelpiece. She could see the card, hand drawn, but not the name. Though she remembered the metal packet of pills. Donipil? Zedonil?

Distracted, she brought out her laptop. The search suggested Donepezil. Catherine hit enter, and cursed.

While she was searching through the facts of the drug, an email came up on her screen. Andy. It was from his private email and contained three photos, obviously from his phone camera of reports on buff paper, hand written, with a Melbourne Zoo insignia embossed on the top left corner.

Dong Zei's last three health checks. Catherine forgot about Bradbury's drug and gave these her full attention. Two were in Beau's handwriting, slanted and thick lettering. His notes covered trunk creasing, eye clarity, work done on feet and temperature. The third was in another hand that was neater and smaller. It discussed the same things, similar blood pressure, weight and other assorted pachyderm vitals.

Catherine wondered if Andy knew an elephant expert who could pore over this with her and look for warning signs or discrepancies. The prospect was slim, so Catherine let her training kick in, and took down the dates, times, and other information in order. These were obviously daily reports, leading into the day of Dong Zei's death. After twenty minutes, she had taken the discussion points of each report. The last report was signed simply S.F. – Simon Forster, she concluded. Beau had signed his whole name. Aside from penmanship and a difference in reporting convention, she found little of interest.

Then she noticed that each form had a catalogue number – Beau's reports on PD-ZD-772 and 773, Simon's report on PD-ZD-775. Catherine checked the dates again. The reports were made on consecutive days. Meaning that a sheet was missing, or had been discarded. Likely on the final day of Dong Zei's life.

10

I'm cheerful; it's the most subtle form of rebellion I can think of.
~ Boris Shakhovskoy

Boris eyed the place from his position at the bar. Tables, chairs, and glass windows punctuated the wooden décor of the Glasgow Palace. Yesterday it was a rough environment that felt like work, like his endless rat wheel. Today, in the quiet, it was paradise.

He looked at the phone again. *'Hope you enjoyed all that tasting last night, let's do it again. X.'*

His knees buckled every time he read it. His face hurt from smiling.

The lunchtime crowd moved in and out, the tip jar kept clinking as people caught his happiness. Covert texting had secured a late night drink after his shift ended. Late night drinks were wonderful for many reasons. In the romantic sense because there was only so much time between good evening and good night, and frankly Boris was so enthralled with the idea of a good night that he could barely spell his own name.

Not that it was purely physical, though if he cared to count how many *Star Trek* movies had come out since last time, he didn't want to count. He felt a genuine, deep and most importantly reciprocated attraction to someone wonderful. Boris didn't need much in life, he was a happy person, yet the idea of someone to share the mornings and evenings with was a cherished idea indeed.

Of course, Catherine provided a wonderful friendship, but they did not, nor ever would they, share a shower or an ice cream. Catherine would never tell him he looked sexy in those pants.

Catherine was at Beau's funeral. Boris couldn't go as he'd taken this shift to be off the night before for Molly. For Catherine, there was nothing he could do but be there, and he couldn't do even that.

Worse, he couldn't even feel that bad about it. The grin wouldn't move. He felt light and tall and powerful. How the hell did he feel fat yesterday, but powerful today? He moved kegs full of beer easily. Even when his break came he wasn't disappointed by his vegie burger – though it still tasted closer to cardboard than anything else. Everything was coloured by Molly. The sky was purple and the air tasted beautiful. It was an exciting time to be alive and be Boris.

Catherine stood as far from the throng as she could. She knew few faces. It wasn't as big a crowd as she would have guessed. Beau being as affable as he had been she had expected a cast of thousands for his funeral. The day had gone colder and the West Brunswick funeral home seemed an inauspicious place for the event. Catherine didn't know who had organised it, possibly Georgia.

She could feel Williams' gaze on her, and had worn sunglasses so he wouldn't know if she was watching him or not. He was standing next to Britt, with his back to Catherine. Even so, Catherine was certain how her jaw was set.

'Hi.'

Catherine turned and found a familiar and unexpected face. Beau's ICU nurse Belinda looked very different in civilian clothes.

'Hi, Belinda. Wow, you must come to hundreds of these.'

Belinda hugged her. Catherine only then realised how lonely she'd felt. Belinda must have sensed it. 'Keep your chin up. Actually, I almost never come to patient's funerals, I just really liked Beau. He had nice friends so I wanted to be here.'

Catherine daubed at her eye with a handkerchief. 'I barely knew him, just a few days. Did I mention?'

'I knew. Someone told me.'

'The police are saying suicide. You said he fought.' Catherine was surprised the words, and the outrage, came out so easily.

Belinda's face was stony. 'Yes, he did.'

'Do you think…?'

She pursed her lips. 'You knew him a few days, so did I. I never heard him talk, and I've seen suicide cases with degrees of intent.'

'What does that mean?'

'It means I don't know. Sometimes there's a duality in people.' She shook her head. 'I'm really not trained in that stuff, sorry.'

They moved towards the entrance as a man in a suit began ushering people in. As the ceremony began, a grey-haired man spoke in a calm tone about a life taken too early. The throng warmed to the routines of a funeral. Phyllis sat up front, handkerchief in hand, with a woman of the same age holding her. It occurred to Catherine she had never asked about Beau's father. A quick scan of the room gave no hints or suspects, though a woman behind Phyllis was almost certainly a sister. The celebrant droned on about Beau's life. A life well lived following a passion for animals. He spoke with a clipboard in his arm. It felt as slick and as genuine as a greeting card.

'The road was at times rocky for Beau. His friends have attested to the tremendous courage he showed in facing some of his trials with fortitude and a look beyond tomorrow. His career will be celebrated for its many achievements and not marred solely by distant or even recent stumbles.'

Catherine's throat made a noise as the room turned red. She turned in her seat, her head jerking to the left. Georgia Potter met her gaze coolly. A hand touched her gently. She turned right and found that Williams was behind her. His eyes were intent on the celebrant, but his finger was still poised to touch Catherine's shoulder. Next to him, Britt gave her the courtesy of making eye contact, shaking her head slightly. Catherine gave her a look that would freeze magma and turned back.

Twenty minutes later, it was done. The coffin was wheeled to the hearse. The celebrant gave directions to the cemetery and Catherine needed a drink more than she had any time in the past century. Belinda squeezed her arm.

'Will you come to the cemetery?'

'No, I'm being observed, and I don't think Beau cares anymore.'

'I noticed you were on the leash. What have you done?'

'What I do. Hey, do you know much about Donepezil?'

Belinda looked over Catherine shoulder, then back to her. 'The Alzheimer's drug? Yes.'

'What can you tell me?'

'It relaxes patients towards the palliative stage. Some people use it earlier to stay sharp.'

'In the early stages, is it noticeable?'

'The drug?'

'The disease.'

Belinda breathed out, dabbing her eye which had stayed dry through the service. 'They say Alzheimer's has six stages until diagnosis and six stages post-diagnosis to death. I know this because Mum had it. There can be years of small mistakes, wandering conversations and general "losing it".' She made the quotation marks with her fingers. 'Do you know someone?'

'I think I may.'

'Then they have a hard time ahead.' She blew her nose. 'My Mum was brilliant before she was diagnosed. I try and remember that and forget the last seven years.'

'Thanks for everything, Belinda.'

Boris had finished cleaning the coffee machine when Catherine walked in looking paler than a vampire moon. Uncharacteristically she was wearing sunglasses. Even before she took them off, Boris knew how her eyes would look. Some people can be right in front of you and still closer to Jupiter than Earth. Her eyes were dull, still, and when they did move, seemed to be getting used to the light on this strange planet.

'Tea or gin, boss?'

'You know Boris,' she spoke slowly, moving her bag onto the bar and leaning against it momentarily. 'I think what is required now is a bottle of champagne, which I think I'll take at the corner table.'

'Was it bad?'

'It was beyond bad. It broke the ninth commandment.'

'Is that the false idol?'

'No. It's the one that goes: Do not bear false witness against thy neighbour.'

Boris handed across the bottle and a glass. 'Oh. A dead neighbour?'

'Yes indeed, and likely buried by now in Carlton cemetery. That made it worse.'

She took a sip, smiled a little. 'I'm not a huge one for biblical scholarship, neighbour's asses being what they are today, but that one seems a big deal. I suspect the whole thing was written by whomever wants to say that he killed himself.'

Boris was focused on something outside. A familiar man with grey hair and wearing a grey suit was standing casually across the street, reading the local newspaper. 'You have company.'

'I thought I might.'

'Should I get a second glass?'

Catherine shook her head. She seemed to be getting closer to earth, metaphorically speaking. Boris would have placed her look somewhere this side of the Mars-Jupiter asteroid belt. 'No. Is he in a car or on the street?'

'Street. He has a newspaper.'

Catherine didn't need to look to know that it was Kenneth Williams. 'Do me a favour, Boris?'

Boris looked back at Catherine. 'Sure?'

'When you have a second, make him a caffe latte and take it out to him as a present from me.'

'Sugar?'

'Two.'

He grinned. 'He doesn't seem the white and two kind.'

'He's not, he drinks it black. It's all I can do to be funny, you see, he hates funny.'

'Got it.'

'I'm going to think about how we fix this now.'

'I'm going to stocktake the chips packets.'

For the next two hours Catherine stared either at the salt and pepper shakers in front of her, or occasionally took out the funeral booklet and looked at Beau's smiling face. The champagne she drank slowly, not getting drunk but "rearranging the furniture inside her head" to quote the great Tom Robbins. In her mind, she played out the scenarios required for the crime to make sense. The gymnast technique that would be required to open the "human" door of the dog's enclosure without being attacked – who could have achieved that? Who would want to? Then there was the matter of who could have organised it, but not done it. People without the physical ability but the clout or the connections to have a job done.

Then there was the party line, uttered by nearly everyone from the first on the scene to the celebrant at the funeral. Catherine pictured in her mind's eye the sight of Beau allowing the door to open as penance for a mistake he could not admit to.

It didn't sit well. Maybe if it had, even for a moment, she could have ordered a strong coffee and gone back to making fine hats. Yet some things, like plaid on paisley, or a tough copper with a milky latte – Catherine had enjoyed watching him pour it into the gutter – will never mix well, no matter how much champagne you pour on top of it.

After a couple of hours Boris took away the empty champagne bottle and placed a gin on the table. Catherine had her notepad out. Boris looked at the scribblings and had absolutely no idea what she was doing.

By eight thirty, when she left the Glasgow Palace, she had theories and had drunk herself sober. She was walking towards the train line, shivering in the chill of the late March night. Williams was long gone, presumably for something more pressing than babysitting a former colleague. Catherine wondered if the surveillance was Britt's idea. Thought better of it. Williams loved to have eyes everywhere on a case, and also loved being those eyes. It was a style of police work that he would never get sick of, even when it pushed him into bullying a civilian.

She fell asleep angry, telling the whole world what to do to itself.

Several hours later she awoke, as was becoming a habit, to the twin vibrations of her phone and her forehead, both of which seemed to be hammering at too great a volume for that time of morning. I will, she said to herself, be a better person, and happily work at a soup kitchen if this call is not from Philomena or the police.

It was from neither, but instead from the veritable font of early morning chirpiness, Nealamber Singh.

'Namaste, Neal.'

'And to you, Catherine. I have decided that since you keep such unpredictable hours that any time is good.'

Catherine nodded as she rubbed her eyes, 'What time is it?'

'Eight thirty, late enough for some of us to have jogged round the block and done some early morning research for a friend.'

She matched his productivity by slumping on the couch. 'You've come a long way since the push-ups of last year.'

'The love of a good woman. Now, the zoo's finances seem to be just as complex and inscrutable as any large organisation.'

'Great.'

'However, they don't seem corrupt. They have roughly fifteen sources of revenue and any number of expenses, but they are doing okay.'

Catherine had blinked eight times in his last sentence. 'Neal. I'm not sure if you've done anything wrong, but I will forgive you anything if you'll come here and make me coffee.'

'If June's aunt wasn't visiting from Bangalore, I would certainly do that. As it is I'm afraid it's an impossibility.'

Catherine swore that Neal's happiness was probably destabilising the world's psychic force some days. 'So, you've had a look and it doesn't appear that there's anything untoward.'

'Or perhaps, in the spirit of good conversation, I was merely saving my punchline for now.'

'I'm awake.' And yes, suddenly she was standing almost straight.

'I'm grateful. What day did the elephant Dong Zei die?'

'It was Saturday, a week ago.' Catherine caught sight of herself in her mirror. It had been a big week.

'That's what I thought. There was a sum of $80,000 transferred on that day to an open fund of Zoos Victoria. There are two interesting things about this.'

Catherine was rubbing her head. 'One.'

'The transfer appears to have been immediately rejected by Zoos Victoria itself.'

Catherine nodded, walking in a small circle around her couch. 'That is strange, what's number two?'

'The funds were transferred by an individual named Ian Bradbury.'

She stopped walking. 'And they were transferred on the very day of the elephant's death?'

'That's right.'

She walked again. 'Interesting. Could be nothing, of course. Though it's interesting. Was there any indication on why it had been rejected?'

'The message, and this took the better part of an hour to unencrypt, was simply: 'Wrong account.'

'Wrong account. So, it could have been going to one of Zoos Victoria's other accounts?'

'It could, but unless I have missed something very important, it has not.'

Catherine caught sight of herself again, chewing her lip and looking no more glamorous. 'And that was a week ago.'

'Indeed.'

This was golden. 'Brilliant Neal, when this gets sorted I will take you, June and as many aunts as you can handle out for a slap-up tandoor.'

'Would you consider dumplings instead? June's Aunt Inderjeet can't get enough of Melbourne dumplings.'

'Done. Good luck with the in-laws.'

He laughed quietly. 'I don't mind. Though it may take a couple of days. Hospitality of relations is a big deal with us.'

Catherine flicked on the kettle. 'In the Anglo tradition we simply ignore and resent each other.'

'I can see its benefits, but I am pro India on this one.'

She ducked her head. 'I take your point. Namaste.'

'Namaste, Catherine.'

The kettle boiled, Catherine chewed her lip. Eighty thousand dollars can buy lots of things. It's a year's wage for middle management or a teacher of a certain tenure. It can buy cars, or the deposit on a house. Catherine was sure that Boris could find very interesting ways of spending eighty thousand, primarily in the form of meals, beer and possibly *Star Trek* memorabilia. Why would Bradbury, already gracing the zoo with his celebrity presence, feel the need to send such a sum on the day of an elephant dying?

She picked up her phone, looking over the texts from Andy showing the health reports of Dong Zei in the three days before his death. On the day she died, Simon Forster had reported nothing of note. On the day she died, Simon Forster had used two health check sheets, entering only one into the records. On the day she died, why would such a large amount of money change hands?

Catherine shot off a text: *Hello insider. What's the chances of Bradbury working late tonight?*

With that Catherine ground some coffee. Today was already feeling better.

11

*You're spiralling towards zero with no hope of anything but blackness,
and no judge to even mark you. I don't know why I'm smiling either.*

~ Catherine Kint

cross town, Boris was wide awake in a house that wasn't his. He
had woken to a different smell than usual and enjoyed a delicious
moment of memory as that previous night flashed past his eyes. He
could hear Molly breathing evenly beside him. The light in her room
was beautiful. There was a well-loved desk in the corner that reminded
him of nothing so much as his own car. It was covered in a snowdrift of
books and papers. She had a bookshelf made in the retro student style
of bricks and wooden boards. He had looked at it groggily last night, a
mix of animal husbandry books, pre-medicine and enough trash fantasy
novels to make his heart sing. This here was a room you could spend a
few lifetimes in.

Catherine's phone buzzed as she sipped her second coffee and read the
weekend paper. It was Andy: *As it's a day ending in Y, probably. If completely
necessary, I shall go to work to confirm. Only if absolutely necessary.* Smiley
face.
  Smiley faces, thought Catherine, nullify all previously pushed
resistance. At least in this case. She texted back to do his duty and then
come visit her with news. That should keep him happy. He replied that
he would go to the zoo, but then had to go to the football, so would
report personally. Catherine was doubly pleased by the response. She

wouldn't have to entertain the charming fellow, and for the first time he wasn't unattractively keen.

The missing report page and the one-off payment seemed a smoking gun, just not one she could place in the hand of any particular individual. What was required was an interview with the donor of such funds to find out what it meant. Catherine looked out her window. She knew she had only a few seconds to make the view bloodlessly. She did. Grey Mazda, four doors down. Man in a suit reading something on his phone. Extra radio aerial on the back. A cop. One of Williams' merry men. He would be there all day; there would be others at the zoo. Catherine finished her coffee and took bread out of the cupboard for toast. It looked like a day in.

'Do you have to go?' Molly looked up at him, morning fresh in her purple dressing gown. Boris was in the clothes he had come in, but was clean after a brief shower.

'If I don't go then all the really special people who live near the pub who call themselves free thinkers and sports fans, but are actually just alcoholics, won't have anyone to pour their beer or hear their latest theory about Marx or Hawthorn.'

'So, you really do then.'

He puffed his chest. 'It's an important job, Molly. One day when you're saving the life of animals you'll reflect on how difficult being a barman is.'

She lay back down on the bed. 'One day when I'm saving enough animals you can stop being a barman.'

Boris knew he would be replaying that soundbite in his head for the next nine hours. 'That will be a great day.'

'Come over tonight?'

He beamed. 'For sure.'

'Bye, honey.' She leaned forward on the bed. He kissed her and went to work. Just like that. A slice of a future he had much desired.

He ran home so he would not keep the free thinkers and sports fans waiting, and so he could have a fresh pair of underpants. That had only become part of his day's plan when he had realised he would see her again that night.

Catherine had a rule: if a hat was not working after forty-five minutes it was time to make something else. That morning she had answered Philomena's one, two, three emails that had gone unnoticed with a progress report aided by photos. This had been met with a phone call where Philomena talked about feeling the work going on and it "making her serene". Catherine managed not to vomit and pushed on for the next forty-five minutes until it just wasn't coming; and so she began working on a series of pillboxes that would be critically overdue in a month if she didn't start now. She was wildly relieved to have a plan that gave her a few hours on her day job.

With the police watching her, she would need to play the defeated milliner who no longer wants to meddle. However, once she had confirmation that Bradbury would be burning the midnight fuel she would enlist Boris and pay a visit after hours. There wasn't much else to the plan, but it felt right. A nice mix of spontaneously questioning someone, breaking into somewhere exotic and potentially making Williams furious. It ticked all the boxes.

At ten past eleven a text came from Andy. *Popped in to clean up emails. Found actual work that needed doing, so thanks. Overheard maintenance crew saying that the lab would be in use late tonight by our "overseas guests". Mission accomplished. Go the Saints.* Smiley face.

Catherine texted back her gratitude with full barracking for the Toronto Blue Jays, Awassa City FC and the social democratic movement. She got nothing back and didn't feel too bad about it at all.

She rang the pub.

'Glasgow Palace, Boris speaking.'

'Ah good, you're in. I need a favour.'

'This, my best friend on earth, is a good day to ask a favour.'

Catherine grinned. 'Did you kiss a pretty girl?'

'I had a lovely night with a *woman*, thank you, my feminist friend.'

Catherine laughed. 'Of course. I'll be up later; what time do you finish?'

Boris was hesitant. 'Finish at seven.'

'Perfect.' Catherine hung up, completely unaware that her best friend's shoulders suddenly sagged.

She spent the rest of the day on the pillboxes, and it was a good day. Sometimes, the mould of the block seems to move easily. After the majority of the week had been taken up annoying people at the zoo, it was a pleasure to be a) alone, b) productive and c) doing something that had clear definition. Regarding the death of Beau, she dealt with more unknown unknowns than anything else. Making hats, they either looked good or they did not, and frankly, these lilac pillboxes looked uniformly fantastic. Some fancy ribbon work and this would be a triumph. At quarter past five she ate a very late lunch and headed to the Glasgow Palace, bowing her head to play the wounded milliner completely given up on crime fighting for the surveillance man in the Mazda.

She had a good feeling about tonight.

'You absolutely can't be serious.' Boris was close to shouting, and several punters turned their heads. They quickly turned back when it became apparent Boris was actually angry and it wasn't his and Catherine's usual banter.

'Keep your voice down, I'm being tailed still.'

'Bloody good thing too,' Boris was vigorously wiping the bar.

'Did you even hear what I said, eighty thousand—'

Boris walked away to serve a customer.

Catherine waited and kept breathing. She was trying to imagine how she could possibly break in without Boris. It was a possibility that she had not previously considered. Boris returned. 'So a rich bloke donates some money to the zoo that's probably paying him a lot of money. It's probably a tax dodge.'

'It got pushed back to him, the day after Dong Zei dies and a few days before Beau was attacked. There's something in this and I can't speak to him through usual channels.'

Boris made a face like someone trying tofu for the first time. 'I have a date.'

'You saw her last night.'

His hand came down on the bar. 'And she wants to see me tonight. Is that so hard to believe?'

Catherine stifled a smile. 'Boris, I want you to hear me.'

'In a second.' He walked away to serve another beer. Honestly, why did Catherine pick 5.30 on a Saturday afternoon to have an ultimatum? While he was, of course he was, running low on change and Jamie was running late for his shift.

The undercurrent was the idea of breaking his arrangement with Molly. He had only known her for a week and Catherine already wanted to ruin it. He focused on the customer, beer served, with peanuts, and a direction to the kitchen for hot chips. Boris returned to Catherine, trying his best to be neutral.

'I'm now listening.'

Catherine leaned in so only he could hear. 'I am thrilled it's going well with Molly. This isn't me sabotaging you. This is me needing your help to do something insane and illegal to find the truth about what happened to my lover. If my gut is right, what we find out tonight will solve the case and you can have the rest of the century to be with Molly.'

Boris gripped the bar. 'You make it sound like I'm breaking up with you. I'm just saying I'm too busy tonight for breaking and entering into a public institution. Can't it wait until tomorrow?'

'No, it can't. I think if we leave this any longer the police will take the soft option and Bradbury will soon after find himself flying to Rio or Pennsylvania or possibly Mercury to be as far away from this as possible.'

Boris leaned in, swallowed the answer, said it anyway. 'You can't bring him back.'

'I can find out what happened. I think I'm the only one who can, and I can only do it with you.'

She turned her head away and wiped her eye. 'That bloke over there needs a pint of pale ale by the way.'

Catherine watched Boris pour the ale. She checked her watch: 6.15. There was time for this. It was strange to see him so torn and she hated doing it, but knew that without him she would be vastly diminished in her chances of success. It was just a matter of time before he came round to the idea. Loyalty was his primary wiring.

He came back. 'Okay. I'll have to make a phone call when Jamie gets here.'

'Good man. Now get me a drink. If I'm still being tailed we'll be in trouble.'

Fifteen minutes later Boris hid in the storeroom with his phone to his ear.

'Hi handsome.' Boris' whole body lurched sideways in happiness.

'Hey you. How was your day?'

'I was studying the whole time, but guess where I am now?'

'Moonlight cinema?'

'I'm at your pub, where are you?'

Boris felt a whole new lurch. 'I'm, um, I'm hiding in the store room so I can tell you I can't come over tonight.' Boris cringed as he said it.

'Oh?' It was a question, which Boris took as positive.

'Yeah, Catherine needs some help with a job tonight. You remember me telling you about her?'

'Beautiful brunette, right?' Molly's tone was unreadable. At least to him.

'Well, she's brunette, I don't know about–'

'About five ten, slim build, hair cut in a bob, wearing tan boots, dark leggings and a black coat?'

'Um, I think…so?'

'I'm sitting next to her. Her drink is empty, you should come back.'

Boris returned to the bar and saw his girlfriend and best friend laughing hysterically about something. He felt a small quiver of relief and a strange certainty that their amusement was him.

He poured a pint of pale ale and made a gin and tonic and brought them over.

Catherine winked at him, pointing. 'Your girlfriend is funny.'

Molly bristled. 'Who's that?' she turned to Boris. 'Who is she Boris, what happened to us?'

Boris could feel his heart actually stop, he could visualise the arteries clogging, and knew that his last moments would be him being accused and ridiculed simultaneously.

They were laughing so hard that Catherine started kicking the bar. Boris could only look at them, as did everyone at the bar. These two women, strangers a few minutes before, set a new noise record as they hooted and snorted. Catherine had tears streaming down her face and Molly was pulling her own hair in an apparent attempt to calm down.

A hand hit Boris' back. 'I'm here man, sorry I was so late. You should knock off. Far out, how much has Catherine had?'

Jamie had finally arrived. Boris looked to the clock and saw it was ten past seven. He was free.

Twelve minutes later they were around a table in the back part of the bar. Molly was finishing her pint and asking questions. 'What's actually the job tonight?'

'Surveillance,' Catherine said quickly. 'I need to speak with someone at the zoo about the death of a friend of ours. I need Boris as a second pair of eyes and ears.'

'Is it dangerous?'

Catherine shook her head, quite convincingly. 'No.'

'Can I come?'

Catherine made a face. 'On this one I really need Boris alone. We've been doing this a long time and he's the best at what he does.'

Molly looked disappointed as Catherine continued: 'Did he tell you about how he saved me from a murderer last year?'

'No.'

'I was tied up with a psycho coming at me with a knife. Boris barged in and saved me.'

Molly squeezed his arm.

Boris looked at Catherine. 'Do you still have company?'

Catherine smiled without humour. 'I think we need to assume that's a positive.'

Molly eyed them warily. 'What does that mean?'

'What that means,' started Catherine with a meaningful look at Boris, 'is that I have asked a few too many questions and now my former colleagues in the police force are trying to make sure I don't ask any more. They've been watching me since yesterday.'

Molly eyebrows knitted and she looked puzzled. 'Why not leave it to them?'

Catherine's voice was still low. 'I think they're wrong.'

'Will you get arrested?' Molly asked Boris.

Catherine shook her head. 'I doubt it.'

Boris stayed silent. This was new territory for him. He had in the past watched Catherine do this with lovers who wanted to "help out" or, more to the point, "keep her home". This was his first time in the situation. It was going appallingly. Catherine gave him another look.

He reached across the table and took Molly's hand. 'I'm sorry. This sounds all very exciting but it's mostly quite boring. We won't be breaking any laws and the only reason there's some urgency around it is because if we don't move now, the case will get closed and one of the suspects will be in Venezuela by Thursday.'

Molly was silent for a moment. Boris was aware cheers from football fans in the front bar were an odd accompaniment to her thinking, but took it nonetheless.

Molly finished her drink. 'Okay.'

Catherine moved forward. 'Okay what?'

'Okay, what you're doing is important. Boris is getting paid?' She eyeballed Catherine who nodded. 'And you're being followed. Right?'

Boris nodded, liking the tone of her voice. Molly continued, 'I just so happen to have my van up the street. It's a nondescript navy transit with no windows. If I go and pick it up I can take it to the carpark out the back and you can dive in. I can drive you to wherever you need to go. In the meantime, you should sit in the window and make it look like you're settling in for an evening on the turps.'

Catherine's eyes widened. Her face practically glowed as she began clapping her hands towards Molly. Boris kissed her. 'That. Sounds. Fabulous.'

Molly got up, excited. 'I'll text you when I'm at the car park. The motor will be running.'

Boris walked her out of the pub. He returned via the bar and came back with a gin for Catherine and a pot – no pints on a working night – for himself.

'Just like you,' said Catherine, raising her glass.

'Just like me?'

'To whinge and moan for years about not finding a girlfriend, then to seemingly pluck the perfect woman out of thin air.'

They clinked glasses. A chorus of football cheers rang out from the front bar.

They had Molly deliver them only as far as Boris' house. On the five-minute journey neither Molly's rear-view mirror or Catherine peering out the crack in Molly's boot window had shown any sign of them being followed.

After a quick goodbye Catherine walked over to Boris' white Ford Laser and watched as he slid various detritus off the passenger seat for her to get in.

Boris started the car as Catherine applied the seatbelt and tried hard not to think about what she might be sitting on. The clock read eight twenty.

Catherine punched Boris' arm. 'You did all right back there.'

'Where?'

'At the pub, not freaking Molly out.'

Boris rubbed his face. 'It all seems normal, doing this stuff. Until you're describing it to someone who doesn't do it.'

'Worse still when that person cares about you.'

Boris' stereo played a tune about targets. He stopped at traffic lights on Melville Road. 'Do you think she would get used to it?'

'Molly?'

'Yeah.'

'Well, if she wants to hang around it's either she gets used to it or we stop doing it.'

He fiddled with the volume. 'It's not like we go looking for reasons.'

Catherine stared at the night. 'No, but we still do it when most people don't.'

They drove on for a few minutes not talking. The night was cool and moonless, clouds blanketed the sky without immediately threatening rain. Boris turned the stereo off. 'It must be worse for you.'

'What?'

'It just occurred to me, I've been single for ages and so no one's ever worried about the danger of going against what the cops want or jumping through a skylight or whatever. I mean, if I told Mum everything I'm sure she'd take a hit out on you, but she doesn't know. This was the first time I've felt like I had to hush it up. You've had several relationships. I wonder how many times a bloke has freaked out about you not just being a milliner?'

Catherine's mouth moved like she was tasting an unsavoury wine. 'Yes, it has come up. Possibly the reason why I'm still single. Still, as I've often said, if a man can't deal with me doing this he's not worth the effort.'

'Beau didn't mind, did he?'

Catherine sighed. 'No, he did not.'

They drove quietly for a minute. Boris tapped the wheel. 'I'm glad we're doing this, all of a sudden.'

They came to the zoo car park. Catherine told Boris not to get too close. A white car marked "security" drove past slowly as Boris killed the lights. Boris looked at the walls.

'That's barbed wire, I'm not so sure the old "Boris gives Catherine a boost" trick will work over barbed wire. Do you have an alternative?'

'I did think of that. There's a heavy rug I've used before on such an occasion.'

'Where is that?'

Catherine cleared her throat. 'Folded neatly in my cupboard at home.'

Boris rubbed his face again. 'Should we go back?'

'No, we're running out of time. I think we should go over the staff gate. There's no wire over that.'

They got out of the car. Catherine took off her coat and placed it in the boot. Boris kept his jacket on. They walked along the rim of the zoo walls, holding hands to give the impression they were lovers out for a walk until they came to the black gates. Illuminated, but with no one in sight. Without a word, Boris crouched and linked his hands, taking Catherine's boot in his grip and she placed a hand on his head and pushed herself over. Boris took a five step run up and was over before you could say flying hippo. He landed heavily, instinctively moving to the darkness at the left of the gate. He found Catherine waiting there. He saw her take her phone and headphones out.

He did the same. She called him and he answered. They kept an ear bud in one ear and the other out, giving them a fighting chance to hear both what was around them and each other. In the years they had been doing this, no one piece of technology had helped more than a mobile phone. It was a game changer, being able to whisper instead of talk, even more so when they were separated.

Catherine indicated the eastern-most set of buildings. They kept to the shadows. At one point Boris heard a click in his ear and froze, a moment later he saw a figure walking in the distance. White shirt, dark sleeveless jacket. Security. They kept moving. Catherine obviously had an idea where she was going. He followed at a distance of five metres. When they came to a door, she signalled to him to watch as she brought out her hat pins. The lock resisted her for about three minutes. Boris heard it click and saw Catherine with her hand on the handle, she then ducked as a light came on inside the building. They moved quickly, Boris to the right, Catherine left, finding shadows with a second to spare.

The door opened and out walked a tall man. He had sandy hair, visible in the light of the doorway, and he walked with a slight stoop. From inside, a voice said something that Boris couldn't make out.

'I'll be quick then,' came the reply.

The man walked rapidly towards a building to the south of them.

After thirty seconds Boris heard Catherine in his earpiece. 'That's Simon Forster. He's Ian's partner. Try and keep him away. I'll go talk to Ian.'

'Got it,' Boris said from his crouch in the shadows.

'Be careful, he's quite fit.'

'Sounds like a party.'

He watched Catherine move quickly into the building.

Boris went to the building Simon had walked towards. There were no lights on, and Boris hadn't been able to follow where he had gone. He lingered in the shadows formulating a plan. He found a few rocks, figuring that when Simon emerged he could toss them over Simon's head and keep him looking for the sounds on the other side of the darkness while Catherine did her work with Bradbury. He thought about fitness and began looking for an escape route that didn't involve barbed wire.

Catherine moved quickly towards where Andy had described the lab to be, and found a sliding door made of glass. She saw Ian in a white lab coat. He was moving into what looked like a cool room, closing the door behind him, leaving the lab area empty. Catherine slid the door open and slipped inside. Ian had an array of microscopes and petri dishes in front of him. A laptop was open with a spreadsheet on the screen. Catherine took a brief look and understood none of it. For all that Bradbury enjoyed his celebrity status, he was an out-and-out animal geek at heart.

Catherine waited for him on a bench stool. She thought of knocking on the cool room door, but didn't want to surprise him. She kept her breath steady and wondered if he would be horrified to see her like he was yesterday, or pleased as he was days earlier. The door opened. Catherine arranged her features into her most beatific smile.

They could probably hear him scream in Russia.

Boris heard the scream in his earpiece and fell over. He had been crouched down and the shock put him onto his backside. All he could hear now was Catherine talking fast and soothingly. He tried to make out the words, something about not wanting to cause alarm. It was then he noticed a figure starting back from the southern building. It was Forster, carrying something with both hands and walking quickly. Too quickly.

Boris took out a stone and tossed it over the keeper's head. It came crackling down on the other side of him. Forster took a brief look and then kept moving towards the lab. Boris could hear Catherine's continued cooing in his left ear, not much from Bradbury. The interview would be over in disastrous fashion if Boris didn't do something quick. He threw another stone.

This one sailed over Forster's head and hit the ground once before banging into something glass and breaking it. Forster turned to the sound, and almost immediately turned back in the direction of Boris, who froze, wondering if the darkness was camouflage enough. His breath was shallow as he tried to be silent.

Simon put down the box he was holding. He stood tall, head not moving, slowly cracking each of his knuckles. They sounded like teeth grinding small bones. There was silence for a few seconds.

Then Simon ran straight at him.

Boris pelted towards the nearest gate. He bounded it in one, moving into a corridor of concrete, with a far gate ahead of him. He heard Simon call out to stop in a reedy voice and moved to the shadows as he saw the door at the other end of the corridor start to open. He guessed it was the security guard and hurled a stone overhead, hearing another hollow dent as he seemed to have hit a metal bin. The security guard followed the sound, opening the door only a fraction before shutting it again. Then Boris saw Forster coming over the gate he had just scaled. Simon's eyes were on the movement at the other end and he flew past Boris, not even noticing the big man as he bounded in the darkness. He was incredibly fast. Sprinting like a demon and then coming to the door without slowing. To Boris' amazement, Simon took the door in a bound, leading with his hands and vaulting over it in a somersault. The man was more super hero than zoo-keeper. Boris hurled another rock as far as he could to the left. He followed them over the gate and ran hard right, buying Catherine as much time as he could.

'Busted,' he reported. 'I reckon you have five, ten at most.'

He kept running.

Catherine had managed to get Ian to sit down.

'I'm not here to hurt you,' she said, soothingly. 'Do you remember who I am?'

Ian blinked hard, as though he still couldn't believe what he saw. 'You're Catherine. You're not Rachel, and Georgia said you wouldn't bother me anymore.'

'Well, you're right on two counts, and I don't mean to bother you.' Catherine was continuing to smile and be as unthreatening as she could. 'There are a few things I need to know.'

Ian was sweating. 'I thought it was over. You didn't say anything at the funeral, I thought it was over.'

'Just breathe deeply while I ask two questions and I'll be gone.'

He was nearly hyperventilating. Catherine heard Boris say that he was busted and removed the ear bud from her ear. It seemed good manners.

'Question one, why did a page go missing from the reports on Dong Zei's health the day he died?'

Ian coughed. 'What?'

'Simon's report that day had two numbers gone past from the previous health check docket. You were with Simon, I take it?'

He nodded.

'Then why was one report docket discarded that day?'

Ian was quiet for a moment, his breathing still quick. Then he coughed again before saying, 'Spelling errors. I found it difficult writing that day. I was writing the report and made a few mistakes. So, I put it in the bin and let Simon do the write up.'

'Mistakes,' Catherine repeated. 'Everyone makes them, don't they?'

His mouth tightened. 'What are you referring to?'

Catherine got off her seat and walked towards him. 'I mean to say that to err is human. Especially as one gets on in life.'

He had stopped spluttering. 'I honestly don't know what you're saying.'

Too quick, thought Catherine, as she took a breath. 'Ian, I think you're unwell and you don't want anyone to know. I think perhaps you've made a few mistakes. Am I right?'

Ian looked at her as if she had grown a second head.

'Everyone makes mistakes,' he growled. 'What's your second question?'

Catherine was very close to him as she spoke. 'Why did you pay the zoo eighty thousand dollars that day?'

He looked away from her.

'Ian, if you have a disease, there is nothing to be ashamed of.'

He faced her with a steely glare. 'It's just–'

His phone rang. It was loud enough to jolt them both.

Ian looked pointedly at Catherine. 'Yes, Detective Houden?'

Boris knew that Simon would find him, whether it was two or twenty minutes away he wasn't sure. He just knew that he was no match for a man who could do that kind of gymnastics. He heard the footsteps and stopped instinctively. There was silence for a full minute. Catherine sounded like she was getting somewhere, and then a phone rang. It was time to find a way out, quickly.

He stopped outside an enclosure he didn't recognise. This should be the penguins? He looked around, trying to get his bearings. Yep, this should be the penguins, because over there were the wild dogs that had attacked Beau. Right. He scooted over to that cage to make sure, knowing that Catherine was in danger of being arrested with every delayed second.

Canadian snow leopard, the sign said. He squinted, looked around and risked being caught by checking the sign again with his torch. Surely it was really penguins. With the light on, it definitely read: Canadian snow leopard. He was lost. Catherine was in trouble and he was lost at the zoo like a mischievous ten-year-old.

He ran, back-tracking, but looking for something familiar. It didn't help he hadn't been here since puberty. He ran to what he thought was east, knowing that at some point the zoo ran out and he would be able to get to the keeper's area and help Catherine. As he ran past a large open area he could see a figure about one hundred metres to his right, walking in the darkness. It was the security guard, or another one, walking fast towards him.

A minute later, he was near the door he was looking for, another that went back to the keepers' area. It was locked, of course, and the fence was three metres. Boris wondered why it needed to be so high. It hadn't been that big where he had entered the main zoo grounds. Regardless, he was up and over in a minute.

He looked around. There was no light. He was suddenly sure this wasn't the admin area. There was no sign of the building Catherine had broken into. The empty space he envisioned hadn't materialised. There was just plant life and growth that looked like a small jungle. Boris was starting to panic when he heard a low growl.

Catherine moved quietly back as Ian spoke. 'Yes, detective, some strange things. My assistant seems to have been delayed. Could you send a car round? Fantastic. Thank you.' He put down the phone. 'You should go.'

'You didn't tell her.' Catherine was still heading towards the door.

He viewed her impassively. 'I said, you should go.'

'Ian, if something's wrong it's not too late to make it right.'

'You,' he said, gesturing gently with his hand, 'have to go.'

There are certain moments where clichés come true, and time seems to stand still. Boris knew that some philosophers called these the road stones of life. The idea is that within these moments, usually of transition, adrenaline and pain, a human experiences their true self – the truest second of their existence. Examples include Saint Paul falling off his horse, Siddhartha achieving nirvana, everyone on the brown acid at Woodstock. These were rock hard moments in time that marked huge changes for the individuals involved, with ripples felt around the globe.

While not all such moments would have such a wide impact, they are the moments that harden within an individual and make them truly understand the elastic nature of the lesser moments they live through.

As the claw ripped him, Boris was aware of these thoughts. He knew about this cliché: the taste of metal in his mouth, the smell of earth and dung and, above all, the searing pain in his shoulder, as he climbed up the metal fence. He gripped and climbed the fence at a speed that others would have marvelled at. His body was solely focused on the idea of up-up-up. He instinctively kicked back and his foot connected with a jagged set of teeth. The world became a roar that shattered through him.

He kept moving, frantic, silent, ignoring the fire in his shoulder and the wetness on his back. Below, the animal growled, making it easier to keep moving despite the pain. He heard another roar and felt a claw against his boot.

With a final push, he moved his weight to the top of the fence and rested. He had hot tears on his face and metal in his mouth. He was breathing deeply and did not want to move. The air was cool, the darkness of the night overwhelmed him as he noticed, as if for the first time, how beautiful the low crescent moon was. He cradled the fence on both sides, knowing he was out of reach of whatever demon was below him.

The animal quietened down, Boris looked down and saw a big cat of some description in the darkness. He sobbed once. Then kept breathing. He was, most definitely, and only slightly precariously, alive. He was starting to move down the non-cat side when his phone rang. Somehow through all that, the ear bud was still in place.

'Hi.'

'We have to go.' Catherine's voice was intense.

'Yep.'

'Where are you?'

'Near a big cat of some description.'

'Which one?'

'Um,' he saw a sign that had been mysteriously obscured before, 'Sumatran Tiger.' He retched.

'Are you all right?'

'I'm bleeding.'

'Oh Christ. Move to your left if you're facing the enclosure. I'll meet you where the bamboo ends.'

He no longer worried about the shadows, just moved in the night air. He realised his shirt and jacket were soaked, with sweat he hoped. He held his hand up to his face, eyes blurry. He was about to keep going into an open area when a hand grabbed him. Catherine.

She hugged him. 'I could hear you breathing ten metres away.'

'My back is sore.'

'We'll get to that. Police are coming.'

'Oh, bloody swell.'

Catherine looked over her shoulder. 'Let's move to the front exit. There must be a way out somewhere.'

'That makes too much sense.'

They went in a slow circle around the perimeter of the zoo. Catherine pushed Boris towards a path that led south-west.

'Change of plan,' she muttered.

As they trudged along, Boris murmured, 'Can you call for our helicopter?'

'They haven't made one strong enough to carry you. Keep up.'

A shout came from behind and they sprinted to the fence. There was another gate. They swapped their usual positions, Catherine hoiking the big barman up and then following suit. Catherine hit the ground running, peeling off towards the bushland on the right. Boris staggered towards the bushes in front of him. He had just found a spot in the undergrowth when a figure appeared on the wall. Tall, athletic and stooped, it had to be Forster. He jumped down, executing a perfect landing, and began stalking near where Catherine and Boris had parted ways.

In the distance, Boris could hear the sirens of a police car approaching. Simon's figure was puffed up, looking for any clue of his quarry. Boris sank as deep into the shallow underbrush as he could. Simon was scanning, very slowly, from one side to another. His head moved so gradually it was imperceptible. It reminded Boris of what Catherine did sometimes at a crime scene. This fellow had training that went beyond vet school. As Simon came closer Boris went completely still, not even breathing. The sirens got louder, but still a minute off.

Their eyes met. Boris suspected he saw Simon stop moving, then was sure as he sprinted towards him.

The scream of tyres came past, almost collecting the zoo-keeper, who reeled back. Boris' Ford Laser turned one eighty degrees and screeched as Catherine spun the wheel. Boris hobbled towards it. The passenger door flew open as she slowed for him to dive in. As Boris sprawled, Catherine floored the accelerator. Boris steadied himself and sat up. He turned and winced, both at the pain and the proximity of the man running fast behind them. Even with Boris' faded rear number plate he would be a good chance at identifying them.

Flashing blue and red lights filled his vision. Catherine made a hard right, avoiding the police car by centimetres. Catherine pushed the car harder into Royal Park.

'How the hell can we lose them?' Boris groaned.

'Sand trap.'

'What?'

'Sand trap.' And with that Catherine pulled a hard left, taking the car off the road and across the footpath onto the Royal Park Golf Course, killing the lights as she sped up. She drove for five more seconds before pulling the hand brake and coming to rest on a low embankment. She turned off the motor.

'Count to ten, Boris.'

He had got to four before the red and blue lights flashed behind them and disappeared up the road.

They took a minute to breathe. Boris felt like his back was on fire.

'Well,' said Catherine brightly, 'that took us a fair way to escape.'

Boris groaned, then laughed, then groaned. Then dry retched.

'Get me water. Get me beer and get me a freaking kebab.'

'Yes. Sir.' Catherine started the car again, backing up slowly so as not to ruin the fairway any further.

12

I rule with an iron wit.

~ Catherine Kint

Catherine's lounge room was brighter than it usually was at midnight on a Saturday. Underneath the full lights, Boris was breathing deeply and enjoying being alive.

'I think it should be sewn.' It was the second time in five minutes Catherine had said that.

Boris was sceptical. 'Who are we going to get to sew this?'

'My friend Melissa did a degree in vet science?'

'Molly's doing vet science, think this won't freak her out?'

Boris was topless in a wooden chair, towels underneath him to catch the blood that fell in slow drips. For comfort, Boris had a beer in his hand and the remains of a kebab on Catherine's bench.

Catherine had washed his wound and was studying it critically. 'What about some glue?'

'I can't see it, Catherine.'

Catherine moved a mirror to line up with the larger mirror on Catherine's wall. Boris winced. Four deep punctures, getting shallower as it raked from his left shoulder to midway down his back. 'I don't think glue or sewing will do much, it's not like I'm bleeding out. Patch it up and pass me another beer. I'm just lucky she didn't get her teeth in me.'

Catherine came with bandages and a beer, passing it to him. 'As far as commitment to me goes, it's a fair statement.'

Boris drank deep. 'You would have done the same for me.' He exhaled deeply and belched, Catherine let it slide. There must be some concessions after a mauling.

He spoke like an extremely tired man. 'I guess the question is: was it worth it?'

'My five minutes with Bradbury?'

He nodded.

Catherine replaced the mirror to its usual position. 'Remains to be seen. And then there's the other question, of whether we'll be arrested for trespass and interrogation.'

'Oh yes, that.' Boris nodded sagaciously and took another sip.

'Actually.' Catherine flopped onto the couch. She was exhausted too and she hadn't even fought a tiger off. 'You should probably go. If they break down the door now we're both stuffed. If you're at home, I can say I was with a stranger.'

'Who just happens to have an exact DNA match with a known associate of yours. No thanks. I'll stay where the fridge isn't far away.'

Catherine was fast coming down from adrenaline. The sight of Boris topless only added to the descent. She decided to make her next gin a double. She needed more bandages anyway. 'I suspect that in the next few days, Ian will change his story or leave the country.'

'If the perpetrator of Beau's attack had to be athletic, Forster's your man. I've never seen moves like that outside the Olympics or a kung fu film.'

Catherine brought more bandages and began patching Boris' wound. 'If it weren't for the rock solid alibi I would be on the phone to Britt right now.'

'You checked the alibi?'

'Sure did. Rang the uni. He was lecturing. Hey, he might be one of Molly's lecturers.'

Boris groaned as Catherine pulled the tape tight across his back. 'Creepy.'

With that, her phone rang. Not a private number, but not a known contact. Catherine checked the clock, 12.45am.

'This is Catherine.'

'What did you say to him?'

Catherine's face dropped, then hardened. 'Talking to me now, are you Britt?'

143

'Don't play. What the hell did you say to him?'

Catherine lay down. If they were going to arrest they wouldn't call ahead. 'I'm at a loss as to whom you mean.'

'I'm on a burner. Scouts' honour. He won't say who broke in, says he didn't recognise the person he was speaking to. His assistant was ropeable.'

'You should talk to him again. I think he's close to admitting that this isn't as open and shut as you would like.'

'I've given him ample time to discuss everything with me. You're blinkered on this, and it's going to get you thrown inside. How's Boris?'

'What?'

'Blood found at the point of exit. I assume it was him. Or was it you?'

'Him.' She looked at Boris' bandages in the mirror. 'Grazed his knee.'

'You watch yourself, Catherine. Williams won't weep for you.'

Catherine snorted. 'He should weep for Beau.'

'He probably is. Every suicide is a tragedy. You haven't seen what I've seen.'

'So tell me. You're breaking protocol already.' Catherine was aware she was close to screaming. Boris hadn't moved, but was watching her carefully.

Britt was quiet a moment. 'He'd tried before Catherine.' And she was gone.

Catherine put down the phone. Looked at Boris. Tried to smile.

Boris swallowed and put his beer down. He read her thoughts. 'He'd tried before?'

Catherine nodded.

Boris got to his feet and trudged to the kitchen. He drank a long glass of water. 'That's crap.'

'I know.'

'She didn't say when?'

'No.'

'That's crap.' His hand hit the bench, hard. 'Heaps of people, especially men, will try. She can't seriously say that because he did previously that it's not worth checking other options before going to the easy one.'

Catherine was standing, a forefinger digging into the palm of her other hand. 'What if I'm wrong?'

'Then why did Bradbury almost confess?'

She shook her head, aware she was trembling. 'That wasn't to Beau.

That was the elephant.' Her eyes filled with tears. 'You could have died, and I could be wrong.'

Boris spoke gently. 'I didn't die. And if Bradbury made a mistake with the elephant then why would Beau kill himself?'

Catherine suddenly didn't want to drink anymore, possibly ever. She was completely numb. 'Because everyone said it was him. Because he'd tried it before.'

Boris took a deep breath, and then a swig of beer. 'Catherine, you're doing something stupid.'

Catherine's voice was quiet. 'Am I?'

'Yes, and I've never seen you do it before. I'll let it slide, provided it stops now.'

'What is it?'

'You're listening to their bullshit. You're letting them get to you.'

'You've let her get to you.'

'What? No I haven't. It's just a—'

'Just a frigging tiger? A tiger Boris!' Molly looked dangerously like she was about to throw the mug she held in her hand. It was morning, with the light streaming behind her in the kitchen. Her oversized coffee mug, which had "Who's the boss?" written on it in bright red colouring, was in her hand. Boris hoped it stayed there.

'Catherine didn't throw me in the tiger's enclosure. It's just—'

'You wouldn't have been there without her. This is just apparently "what you do",' she made aggressive punctuation marks in the air. 'It's a terrible friendship. You're either her surrogate boyfriend or sidekick about to get eaten. How could this possibly be okay?'

Boris looked around, aware of her sleeping housemates, who probably weren't sleeping anymore. His hands were out in a conciliatory pose. 'But I am okay and we can talk about this, but I need you to know that I'm really okay.'

'This time.' She jabbed a hand towards him. 'This time, you're okay. It's just another funny story to tell at the pub, Boris and Catherine, woohoo, but what about next time?'

Boris spread his hands wide. 'Who knows if there will be a next time?'

'How did you get that scar?'

'Which one?'

'The side of your face, that one, at the line of your beard.'

Boris stood taller. 'Now I don't think that's got anything to do with–'

'How did you get it, Boris?' The mug was in throwing pose again. 'I don't know and I'm interested. It's a reasonable question, don't you think?'

'Reasonable.'

'How? Tell me.' She spat the words with a venom Boris didn't think possible on a Sunday morning. He was about to yell. He could feel the words welling up and then he saw the tears. She put the cup down on the kitchen bench and wilted in front of him. Sobbing.

He went to her, though she exploded with limbs. 'Don't touch me.'

For the next two minutes, she sobbed on the floor, him hunched over her desperate for a way of fixing it so they could laugh and go back to bed. A few hours of sleep at Catherine's place had done little to rest him. He was desperate to sleep, but had been more desperate for her not to worry.

The hero's welcome he was expecting hadn't gone to plan.

After a few more minutes, she looked up. 'I was so worried.'

'I'm sorry, honey.'

She let him hold her. She buried her face into his shoulder and he winced as she held onto his back.

'I've hardly slept I was so worried.'

'You should have texted.'

'I thought I might have blown your cover.'

They looked at each other, brimming, and then giggling. The laugh went for a few seconds, quavering and vulnerable.

He put a hand behind her head. 'Let's go to bed, I'm pooped.'

They moved down the hall together. She spoke in a quieter voice. 'How did you get that scar, Boris?'

He was silent a second, then said, 'I fell through a skylight.'

'Was Catherine there?'

They were at her bedroom door. 'Yes.'

'I don't think she's a very good friend, Boris.'

'Let's just sleep, honey.'

Catherine awoke on the couch to the sound of an empty apartment. No Boris in the bedroom – getting mauled by a tiger means you get the only bed, it's the rules – not even Minty waking her up. She smiled to herself. If Boris had a girlfriend, this was the new normal. She allowed herself to feel sad for a minute, knowing that it was perfectly understandable. He had stained her sheets with blood, but this too would be tolerated under the circumstances.

Catherine switched on the kettle and swore silently that she had missed two calls from Philomena. Catherine shook her head and walked out to the balcony into the chill of the autumn. Only to shiver as she saw who was waiting for her.

Philomena Kaboru stood on the other side of her road peering up at her. She held up a takeaway coffee cup in one hand, another against her side.

'I thought you might need a double this morning.'

Without a word, Catherine was back inside. As she went down each stair she could feel the bile rising in her throat. She threw open the front door.

'Philomena.' She marched across the street. 'Even the "gift" crap aside, you can't stalk people.'

Catherine suddenly realised her hypocrisy. She hoped it didn't show on her face.

Philomena looked at her hard. 'I am bringing you coffee because you are alive. Last night I wasn't sure if you would be. Something about an animal.'

'Shh,' Catherine looked around, hoping Williams' little helpers weren't anywhere close. 'Aside from the damned hat, which will be done on time, it shouldn't matter what I do when.'

Philomena tried to smile. 'Perhaps I haven't told you how important—'

'I get it's important. It's my business, so it's important to me too, but until I ring you about the hat. Please. Please.' She punctuated this with both hands chopping the air. 'No more texts, no more phone calls. Unless you sense I'm on fire and you happen to have an extinguisher, leave me alone. Please,' she added for good measure.

Philomena chewed her lip as if weighing up an answer. 'All right. No contact. Will you take the coffee?'

Catherine grabbed it. 'Yes, I think I will, thank you.'

Catherine went upstairs trying to calm down. There should be a surcharge on customer neediness. She sipped the coffee, which was irritatingly delicious and exactly how she liked it.

It was nine thirty. Philomena would only disappear when the hat was done, and there was nothing more she could do about the zoo. Boris hadn't been eaten. Catherine had done a reasonably good job at the zoo last night. The ball was in Bradbury's court. He would either listen to his conscience, or be damned to have her reminding him about it until he did. Either way, she would give him a few days to think about it. She was persistent, but not a psychopath.

The green hat was getting close, and yet the back angle came across as clunky faux-science fiction. She stared at it, turned it, stared at it more. Waiting for the genius to hit her, that it was perfect, waiting for the knowledge that her toil was worth it to fill her through her gut. She looked for fourteen minutes; her gut did not move. Intellectually it worked, but it lacked something. If she knew what that something was, she wouldn't be spending a Sunday morning looking at a green, three tier act of imperfect fashion, waiting for it to redeem itself.

Her phone rang: Neal.

'Neal, I swear every time I want to speak with you, you ring. Have you become psychic?'

'No, I'm desperate to get away from Aunty Inderjeet. If I am asked one more time about when the babies are coming I will scream.'

Catherine laughed. 'Family. Who would have them?'

'Usually I love the idea, but today I'm all for autonomous cloning. Now if ever June or Inderjeet ask, you pay me lots of money to do this work right? Lots of money.'

'Piles, truckloads.'

'Good lady. I have found very little, but the little seems of great significance. What was that first rule of politics you always espouse?'

'Never create a scandal the public can understand?'

'That's it. I couldn't recall. Well, a good thing Mr Bradbury is not a politician. I have found the last resting place of his eighty thousand dollars.'

'Whores, drugs?'

'A woman named Georgia Potter, whose professional website tells me she is chairwoman of the zoo board.'

Catherine struggled to hold on to the glass she had forgotten she was holding.

'Neal, you're brilliant.'

'So I'm told. Another thing, Catherine.'

'What?'

'I looked into Ms Potter's accounts. The money is already gone.'

Spent on power suits and ivory, Catherine imagined.

'You're the best, Neal.'

With a plan formulating, Catherine went back to the hat. That wonderful hat, those wonderful sails. Why make sails look more like a hat, when you could…

It was done in fifteen minutes. Catherine was fit to burst. It was the best work she had ever done. It would flow, streamlined, across the wearer's hair. It looked like the idea that nature was going to have next.

She ran a shower to celebrate.

Boris winced as he got out of the shower, gritting his teeth against the cool on his broken skin. He had winced getting in as well, and was now grimacing as he towelled himself, trying not to get blood on Molly's blue and yellow beach towel.

Molly walked in and kissed him. 'Feeling all right?'

'No worries.' He had a moment, while looking for his underpants, of pure happiness as he realised he was naked with her and it felt great. One day he might even stop sucking in his gut.

'Do you have to go to work?'

He winced as he put a leg in his jeans. 'Similar story to yesterday.'

'Ah yes, the sports loving alcoholics. Aren't some of them union people? Shouldn't there be a law against working the day after you've been mauled?'

Boris puffed out his chest. 'Oh, you were pretty gentle really.'

Molly threw a comb at him. He ducked, then grimaced. 'I'll get someone else to do the heavy stuff . You could come in?'

She smiled and looked back to the main room. 'No, much as you're irresistible. Part of me just wants you all afternoon because you're more fun than bovine heart irregularities.'

He paused as he put his shirt on. 'That's the nicest thing anyone's ever said to me.'

His phone rang, and Molly's face changed. He turned it off as he saw the name.

Molly was looking at him as his expression grew sheepish.

'What's she want now?'

Boris dropped his gaze and suddenly wanted to be at work and eating a hamburger. 'She's in a fair bit of pain right now. Her fella just died, y'know?'

Molly straightened his collar. Kissed him.

'I know,' she said sadly. 'You'd think that would make her more careful with someone else's.'

'Aw babe.'

Molly, resigned, said, 'I won't see you for days now. Try and not let her kill you.'

'Babe.' His mouth was working overtime. He could feel the tension in his jaw and his legs as he tensed against the bathroom floor. 'Look, I can't make you know her, but she's a great friend. How about I come to uni with you tomorrow? I have the day off.'

'For canine biodynamics and husbandry?'

'Sure, sushi and falling asleep in a lecture theatre, I got a degree in it.'

She loosened a bit. 'First lecture at ten, last one at four. The rest of the time you can help me in the library.'

They were walking through her hallway. 'I was thinking more like sleeping in the student lounge.'

She finger-gunned him as he walked to the gate. 'Pick me up at nine, handsome.'

Boris walked to the pub, feeling like he'd danced on a pinhead. He started to call Catherine, but his pace slowed. He thumbed the phone and felt how much his back was hurting. He put his phone in his pocket and kept walking.

Catherine had stared at the hat for a full five minutes before she called Philomena. For the first time, she got her voicemail. Ten minutes later she got the voicemail again. She left a message that the hat would be ready ahead of time.

It really was spectacular. Catherine realised a growing doubt that it would perhaps never be paid for. Perhaps Grace had hired Philomena as a psychic in order to mess with Catherine. Catherine comforted herself with the certainty that this green wonder would take pride of place in any number of magazines.

The idea of Grace wearing it made her stomach churn. Speaking of, she was hungry, a breakfast was certainly in order. Everything needs to eat, digest and…a thought came and her throat caught.

Suddenly, Catherine had found a way to maybe, just maybe, have a win.

It took a full half hour, by which point she was starving but the hat still looked superb.

After breakfast at the tender hour of three in the afternoon, Catherine walked home. She pushed her face up to a window of the Glasgow Palace but there was no Boris to be seen. She tried his number, no answer. Probably still sleeping, possibly with Molly.

'The new normal,' she said to herself quietly and tried to feel happy for him.

She was almost home when the phone rang again. Not Boris. Private number.

'This is Catherine.'

'This is Brittney.'

Catherine took her keys out of her bag as she climbed the stairs to her door. She could hear Minty scratching on the other side.

'Hello detective.'

'Catherine, this is a courtesy call.'

Catherine put her bag down and walked into the light of her house. She had left the heater on and enjoyed the warmth.

'What was last night?'

'That was a friendship call.'

'Right. I won't enjoy this one as much?'

She heard Britt sigh. 'Catherine, tomorrow I'm declaring the case finalised. I found no evidence to contradict the theory that Mr Hacska either deliberately or mistakenly allowed the dogs out of the door, resulting in the attack.'

Catherine leaned against a brick wall, steadying herself. 'Oh, so you're leaving wriggle room in the suicide theory for him to just be a plain dickhead then, are you?'

'Catherine.'

'Really playing all the angles, aren't you?'

'Catherine. You should have seen his file. He tried to hurt himself twice before, both times when things were going badly professionally.'

'When?'

'I'll be able to talk about it more after we've finalised…'

Catherine stamped her foot. 'If I get courtesy calls and friendship calls you're either my friend or you're polite! Answer the question! When?'

'Both times were not recent, however—'

'It's convenient! And it's your first case, and you get to do it quickly and show Williams that you can do it even when I'm snapping at your heels.'

'I'm right Catherine,' Britt was calm. 'This isn't a quick win; this is an easy case.'

'Did you look into the finances of Bradbury or Georgia Potter?'

'I found nothing that implicated anyone in this case. I asked questions and they answered. Now I have said more than I wanted to already. Let's talk in a few days.'

Catherine fumed, and was lost for words.

'Catherine?

'Yes?'

'Don't drink too much?'

Britt hung up, so she had no idea that Catherine threw her phone across the room.

13

It's very frightening when the person you know becomes inverted.
You wonder if you have dreamed a great love and projected it onto a monster's face.

~ Phyllis Hacska

It was difficult to get up the next day, despite the lack of hangover. Catherine watched the light change in her room for what felt like a long time.

When she was seventeen she'd had shingles. It had left her bedridden for two weeks. Afterwards, this event had no bearing on her life. Then she had broken her arm aged twenty. Six weeks in a cast, no bearing on her life after taking it off. Years later, no one cared.

Had she had a manic episode, however, it would have been remembered, leaving those around her to wonder if, or when, another episode may happen. Depression seemed to be more accepted as something that happened to "normal people", and not treated as something that lingered. Anything involving self-harm however, or hospitalisation, or arrest, and you were seen differently. Not necessarily punitively, but there was always a worry in the eyes of others that you may again "turn".

This happened because of fear. Shingles and broken arms don't usually change a person. You can buy them a get well card and have a cuppa on the couch. Mental illness scares people. It robs them of the certainties they have about someone they care for. The person may ask questions you can't answer. Repeatedly, they may act in ways that are distasteful. They may beg you to help them escape the hospital you've just spent three hours getting them admitted to.

They may hurt themselves, they may hurt others, they may hurt you.

The fear is understandable, the judgement unacceptable. Someone having a mania is as incapable of "snapping out of it" as someone with the broken arm can play table tennis. It's a matter of healing, time and patience.

Then there was the matter of this particular case, when a man had gone through trauma and came out a ridiculously well balanced thirty-two-year-old, only to have his possible murder written off because his file says he was once, and therefore was forever, a crazy person.

Being a potential suicide, the story wouldn't go to the press. It would be dropped and never be touched by the media unless Beau's family agreed to the story being explored in some "suicide awareness expose".

Catherine thought she should get up. Make hats. Forget about it. She decided she would. Later. Right now, she would allow herself the first sleep-in she'd had since yesterday. Brittney could screw the case up; Beau wouldn't come back. At least Catherine could sleep and leave the working stiffs to their Monday mornings. They could all go and–

With a jolt her phone practically screamed at her. Her throwing it the night before must have pushed the volume up to biblical. Catherine was sitting upright and snorting in a way that seemed unladylike even under the circumstances.

'This is Catherine.'

It was a material supplier. Catherine groaned, and tried to feel normal.

'Did you get any of that?' Molly returned to him with two paper cups of coffee. Hanging off her shoulder was a satchel carrying a few readers and an iPad.

Boris, who had worn his lucky shirt for the big day back on campus, puffed out his cheeks. 'I don't know if it's because I'm older, but I have never been so confused in a lecture in my life. I'm sure more of the words were in Klingon than English.'

She passed him the drink and sat down. They stared across one of the beautiful gardens on the university campus. The view was mostly taken up by a bunch of bright young things sitting under trees and ignoring each other. 'Don't fret. It's a third year subject and I suspect you gave science a miss from say, Year Ten?'

'Guilty.'

She scrunched up her face. 'Why do sci-fi boys never get into the exact science?'

'It wasn't so much the quantum as the story that gets us going; hence the arts degree.'

'Come up to the lab, I'll show you something hot.'

'Sounds great.' He paused. 'Is it a Bunsen burner?'

'Yep.'

Boris slowed his getting up, 'Oh, all right.'

Catherine made hats for the day. She took four phone calls from clients, none of whom seemed to be irritating or psychic, and sent an email to Philomena with photos of the finished green hat from three angles. It was a usual Monday.

Catherine gave no thought to the fact that there was no reply from Philomena. Many a client conveniently disappeared for a few days after a job was completed. Surely it was nothing to worry about. Not when there were other things on her mind. Things she couldn't switch off.

Catherine was certain that Beau hadn't wanted to hurt himself. If only because she was the last person to share a night with him and he wasn't suicidal. Nor was he addled, confused, or even particularly overtired. Every time she remembered him, she remembered a happy man. A contented person. Someone who loved animals and had worked with zoos in at least two countries. He was not suicidal.

Despite that, the police had decided that he was. Even a good cop, and her friend, had decided that he was. Or it was a death by misadventure. It sounded fun until you fully understood it involved a death.

'The least I can do is apologise to him.'

Catherine said the words, but did not understand where the thought came from.

In the corner, Minty stretched and pawed the carpet. Catherine looked at the email she had half written regarding a brim length, and abruptly closed her laptop. For the first time in days she knew exactly what to do.

She'd left the house and gone half a block when she turned around. It was the first cold snap of the approaching winter and her Vespa was unbearable without gloves. Back on the road and protected from the chill, the traffic was relatively easy. In twenty minutes she had parked the Vespa and was walking through the gates of Carlton Cemetery. She was beginning to feel ridiculous. The resolve from earlier was gone. This was pure sentimentalism.

Catherine hadn't gone to the grave site three days earlier due to the lingering presence of Williams. Today, she'd walked aimlessly before realising the limited real estate left on this holy ground meant she should just search for the newest looking graves. There weren't many. She didn't know what denomination he was, it hadn't come up, like so many other details. She increased her pace, if only to warm herself up.

The cemetery was quiet. A couple of students from the nearby university walked through carrying books and talking quietly. An elderly lady left flowers on a grave nearby. Catherine was walking into the light of the descending sun, bright even through the clouds. So she had to blink a few times before she noticed the shape of the man walking towards her.

'Oh God. Not again.'

'Sorry.' Catherine blinked again. The features came together. A man Catherine felt like she had known all her life, even though she had only met him a week earlier.

'I'll tell Detective Houden this time.'

Catherine put up her hand, and kept walking. 'This one's coincidence, Bradbury. I'm here to see someone else.'

'Oh.' He put his hands in his pockets. 'You're here to see Beau.'

'Yes. Do you...?' she left it hanging.

'I'll show you. He's over here.'

They walked together in silence for a minute.

'Just paying respects?' Catherine asked him.

Ian nodded. 'Detective Houden told me her conclusions.'

'Me too. I was coming to say sorry.'

They approached a grave. Beau, it appeared, had joined some relatives in the westernmost area of the cemetery. There was a view of Princes Park. Even in the cold it was beautiful.

'Sorry?' repeated Ian. 'That seems a funny thing for you to say.'

Catherine looked at him and did not see an evil man. She turned to Beau's small plaque on a family stone. 'I don't think I know what happened. I wanted to but I didn't. I feel like I failed him. I came to say sorry.' She shrugged, and put her hair behind her ear. 'It was all I could think of doing.'

They stood in silence. Catherine could see Ian's right foot was at an angle to the rest of his body. His foot wanted to walk away. After a while he spoke again. 'You talked about doing the right thing the other night. I haven't stopped thinking of that.'

She gave him her full attention as he stood with a foot each way.

'Ian, do you know who killed Beau?'

His face was impassive for a few seconds, then his lips flickered and his eyes dropped. 'No.' His eyes slowly came up to her face as he steeled himself. 'But I know who killed Dong Zei.'

A tear trickled down the left side of his face.

'Bring your voice down, detective. Yes, she's with me. I can't see how that changes anything. We need to talk. I need to tell you a few things.'

Catherine couldn't hear the response from Britt, but Bradbury winced a couple of times that made Catherine think of Boris post-Saturday night. 'No, I really do. Bring Georgia too. If you're at the zoo we'll meet you at the Japanese garden. Georgia needs to hear this as well. If it needs to go further, we'll go from there. Let's do it now. I'll bring Catherine.

'No, she deserves to be there. I insist. We'll see you in ten minutes.'

He shoved his phone in his pocket. 'There's no going back now.'

Catherine put a hand on his shoulder. 'You've not hurt anyone.'

'I've broken a few rules, at least my own.'

He stood straighter than Catherine had seen him stand. 'Come on. Walk an old man to his reckoning?'

He held out an arm. Catherine took it. They started walking. Ian paused and pulled out his phone. 'There is one other person who should know about this.'

Boris had, after two hours of watching Molly in the lab and thinking about many inappropriate uses for lab coats, enjoyed one of his favourite university experiences: a couple of pints over lunch. As he and Molly looked over the north court, he felt a strange nostalgia for the years he had spent there, when he had only dreamed of getting away. Molly looked like she was packing up ready to leave.

'Another?' he said hopefully.

'Ha, slacker. Remember the four o'clock lecture.'

'Surely there'll be a podcast. Look, there's going to be cheap pizza soon; I saw the Beer Appreciation Club were putting it on.'

'Come on. Maybe you'll understand four words this time.'

Boris got up wearily, suddenly sleepy and worried about his bladder control over the next fifty-seven minutes.

Molly set a brisk pace. 'You'll like this lecturer; he works at your favourite place.'

'He works at your house?'

She smiled. 'No, he's a keeper at the zoo, totally eccentric.'

'What's his name?' Boris asked, looking out for a bathroom.

'Simon Forster.'

'I wonder if this is necessary. Detective Houden was briefing me on the findings.' Georgia Potter was speaking extremely fast. 'It's an unfortunate business, but it's done. What do we need to rehash, Ian? What good will it do?'

Catherine was glad to see Britt blink at that.

Ian seemed diminished again, but drew a deep breath. 'I need to discuss a few things with the detective that seem to have slipped my mind earlier.'

'Before you go on, Ian.' Britt was close, with her shoulder suddenly cutting Ian off from Catherine's sight. 'I need to be assured that you haven't been coerced or bullied into making further statements, because perverting the course of justice is a serious charge.' She looked pointedly over her shoulder at Catherine. 'As is coercion.'

Catherine scoffed. 'My God, would you just take yourself a little less seriously, detective? You're sounding more ridiculous than the whole aviary.'

Britt rounded on Catherine. 'I've had about enough from you–'

Ian was almost shouting. 'Detective. Please. I have Alzheimer's disease.'

Britt's head jerked towards him. 'What?'

'I,' he looked at Catherine, who smiled. Georgia was suddenly looking down. 'I was diagnosed a few months ago. I'm on a relatively radical treatment. Though I wonder if a side-effect hasn't been utter, utter stupidity.'

Britt squared her shoulders; Catherine was no longer on the outer. 'I'm listening, Ian. Is this regarding the death of Mr Hacska?'

'Possibly, though it starts with the death of Dong Zei.' He took another deep breath and then squinted as if he saw something.

They were late to the lecture due to Boris' bladder. They had to walk over two other students to get to the only two seats left in the auditorium. Boris apologised, but secretly hated them for not moving to the middle of the row. What the hell did they think was going to happen? The lights were low, for some reason. They had been bright in the early lecture. Boris wondered if Simon would be as boorish as that dry white toast professor had been. He was also wondering if he could possibly fall asleep quietly enough so as not to bother Molly when his pocket vibrated. He checked the text message. Catherine: *Your valour is not wasted. Bradbury is confessing to the manslaughter of Dong Zei now at the zoo. I couldn't have done any of this without you.*

Boris leaned back in his chair. Wow, Catherine was right. Dong Zei wasn't Beau's cock-up and he could have his reputation back posthumously. It didn't explain who had killed Beau, but Boris couldn't imagine Bradbury could have avoided the dogs if he had opened the door. Only the young outrun tigers, he smiled to himself.

At the front of the lecture theatre a screen rolled down slowly. As if a projection was about to start. When the video began, Boris didn't see the canine anatomy he was expecting, but the face of a man. A man who had chased him into the cage of a Sumatran tiger forty hours earlier.

'It's a video?' he whispered to Molly.

She scowled back in the darkness. 'Yeah, it's always a video.'

'You mean every time Simon Forster does a lecture it's videoed?'

'Shh, yes.'

Boris swallowed. This was Foster's rock solid alibi. The lectures were on, but they were filmed. Meaning that most athletic man, who could have orchestrated Beau's murder, did not have an alibi at all. He suddenly needed the bathroom again.

And Catherine was in the zoo, with his mentor, who was confessing to a major mistake, with criminal implications.

'I have to go.'

'You just went,' Molly spoke between gritted teeth.

'No, I have to go to the zoo. Catherine's in trouble.'

She turned her face fiercely. 'What?'

Some students turned and tutted.

'I'm sorry honey, I have to.'

'Boris,' she called, too loud, as he fell over the students blocking his way to the aisle, stairway, and then door.

Bloody uni students, he said to himself as he ran.

14

People are remembered either for their triumphs or their mistakes, whichever is catchier.

~ Simon Forster

As the blood spattered over her, it occurred to Catherine that while she had tended dozens of bodies, she had never – up until now – watched someone being shot. It wasn't anything like the movies.

Seconds earlier, Ian had blinked and then pushed Catherine and Britt away in opposite directions. Falling backwards, Catherine had watched as he yelled, 'Simon.' Then winced in anticipation of the bullets that ripped into his chest.

Catherine only moved a few metres before catching her footing. She looked up and ducked instinctively as she saw Simon's arm rise. The gun sounded louder this time. Deafening. Whether the bullet missed her by centimetres or millimetres she would never know. As unknown arms pushed her weakly to her right, she went with the movement. Her gaze flicked back, past Ian's body, to where Brittney drew her gun.

She's never fired it, came the thought, a second before Britt's gun discharged. Catherine realised that the person pushing her was Georgia. The woman bustled her towards a grey steel wall.

Simon's gangly frame ducked behind a picnic table he had pushed over. Britt stood tall over Ian's motionless body. Her stance was as strong as her position was vulnerable. Catherine screamed her name as Georgia fumbled with keys. Catherine saw Simon pivot and pulled Georgia down as a bullet slammed into the steel door they were against. Georgia shook off Catherine and pulled the door open, dragging it against the branch of a magnolia tree. Catherine followed her. Georgia slammed the door as Britt's weapon fired again.

They were in a small cupboard, built into the wall of the building. There was little light. Catherine could smell the dampness of a mop. Georgia crouched beside her. Catherine noticed the light was coming from a bullet hole at her head height. She swallowed as more shots blasted out in the garden. She steeled herself and brought her eye to the hole. Simon stood against the thick wooden table, which shook slightly with the impact of another bullet.

The hole Catherine looked out of was not large, and her field of vision was limited to a few metres. She could not see Britt immediately, then she could see Britt's arm and wrist holding her gun.

Catherine focused on Britt's weapon, saw it kick once more as she fired, and then move and click, empty. Catherine wondered if Britt held any more ammunition.

Simon had heard the click and moved quickly towards Britt. At that point Catherine's field of vision failed her. All she could see was the garden and Ian's body.

Catherine was suddenly aware of her own breathing, deep and hard, also that of Georgia's, shallow and accompanied by a whimper. Catherine couldn't blame her.

'Is he dead?'

Catherine kept an eye on their newly made peephole. 'No. Oh Christ.'

'What?'

'He's got Britt.' Simon was frogmarching her friend, gun to the head, her hands up, they moved out of sight.

Catherine's phone started ringing. Could be Boris. She checked her pockets. Not there. She listened; the ringtone was coming from the other side of the door. In her mind's eye she could see it, on the ground outside. She swore quietly, but with feeling.

'How do we get out of here?' she asked Georgia.

Catherine couldn't be certain in the light, but her eyes looked wet. 'Here.' Her shaking hands meant the keys rattled.

Catherine fumbled with the keys, and brought her hand down to the knob. It was smooth as marble. She ran her hand up and down in the semi darkness. There was nothing, not a handhold, not a latch, just a small round knob where the keyhole was on the other side, nothing that a key could fit on the inside. 'Are we supposed to be able to get out of this?'

'I'm not sure.' Georgia stood up in the confined space. 'I didn't design the place. I just run the admin.'

Catherine gave up. 'Well, your African dogs can get out, but your mops are absolutely secure.'

A stream of people were moving quickly from the zoo. A tall man in a denim jacket practically flew along pushing a toddler in a stroller with a frizzy haired schoolgirl running beside him.

'I wouldn't go in there, mate,' he yelled. 'Gunshots.'

'Thanks, mate,' Boris yelled as he passed. He pounded through the front entrance and hurdled the barrier. The place was almost deserted. He realised he had almost no idea where he was going. Then he heard a gunshot coming from the area of the food court and headed that way. He saw three keepers huddled behind a food van, one with a phone to her ear. Whatever was happening, police would soon arrive.

He pushed on, thinking he really should stop and find out where Catherine was, and that he should have had a third pint just in case he got shot. He was coming around the red panda enclosure when he heard a voice, charged the blind corner and hit two people full pelt. Then he heard the gunshot, as loud as a bomb. So close he could smell the powder.

He saw a flash of bodies, a streak of blonde hair and then went down, his knee catching someone's legs as he went. He felt something crack under it. Then a pain went right through his chest.

A woman screamed and he looked up to see Britt sprawled on the bitumen, her right ankle at an unnatural angle. She was screaming with her mouth closed, her hands cupped her leg above the break. Simon was also on the ground. The pain in Boris' chest spread. He felt for holes, and realised that he wasn't shot but winded. Simon snarled and went to stand, wincing and grabbing at his side as he stood.

Boris tried to get up and punch him, got about two centimetres off the ground, saw the black butt of the gun and felt a thunderclap on his face. Boris reeled from the blow and wet himself, just a little. Then, his hair was pulled and he was up before he knew, with a gun under his chin, staring at Simon, who looked blurry.

'You're with the pest? Aren't you?' Simon's voice was light.

Boris' everything hurt. He thought of Molly. 'Five nights a week, dickhead.'

'Let's go.' Simon threw him forward. Boris, just able to keep his feet, turned to see Simon point the gun at Britt. 'You up or you dead?' His tone wasn't conversational. Boris lifted Britt and held her up as they hobbled in the direction that Simon pushed them.

Boris thought they were going out the north entrance. His phone rang. He didn't answer, figuring it would be bad for his health. He could see no people, could hear no sirens. Where the hell was everyone? He moved as quickly as he could, Britt hobbling beside him on the grass of the picnic lawn.

'Fatty!'

Boris looked at the thin keeper with the gun then said to Britt, 'I think he's talking to you.'

Simon tittered.

Britt shook her head, a warning not to be cute.

Boris turned back to Simon. 'Yeah?'

'Carry the cop, we have to move.'

'Where?'

'There.' He pointed with his left hand, his right hand holding the gun on Boris.

The reptile house.

Boris' sore face creased. 'What?'

Simon smiled sweetly. 'Carry the cop or I'll shoot her.'

Boris picked Britt up and carried her, fireman style, over his shoulder.

'Now we run. Keep up or you're both dead.'

Boris pushed his legs, sweat blinding his eyes. Britt was shaking. She knew how to be carried, going limp and adjusting her weight. Boris wondered if she'd had training. It occurred to him that Catherine would be useless at it, likely criticising his technique in the same circumstances.

Within minutes, they were outside the reptile house. Simon began opening the roller doors. Boris panted, doubled over, as Britt stood on one leg then hobbled towards the doors. The way she was grunting told Boris she was in considerable pain. He saw the dim light of the reptile house and suddenly wanted to see Molly, just once more. Tears came to his eyes as he looked at Simon's gun. It was pointed in his direction as Simon spoke to himself. 'When the student is ready the teacher appears. The teacher gives meaning. Such a wonderful man. He loved animals so much.'

Simon ushered them in with a wave of his gun, his face impassive. 'In we go. It's my favourite part of this place.'

Catherine had tried picking the lock with hair pins, which didn't work because there was no lock on her side. Then she attempted bashing the doors, then dismantling the hinges – which she should have tried before she bloodied her fist – then wedging the mops underneath to jam the door. None of which worked even slightly. She had yelled, screamed and was properly upset.

She leaned against the doorway. There was hardly any room.

She watched, in the almost blackness, as Georgia rocked on her haunches. 'How much did you know?'

Georgia looked up. 'What?'

Catherine's voice was irritable, even to her own ears. 'Well, if the bad guy comes back we could both be killed, so give me the satisfaction. How much did you know?'

'I didn't think anyone had killed Beau. That I swear.'

'What about the elephant?'

A gunshot rang out in the distance. Georgia gave a sob and was shaking again.

Catherine steeled herself. 'The elephant, Georgia. Dong Zei. What happened?'

Georgia's voice was small. 'He screwed up.'

'Who, Bradbury?'

She was crying now, talking between sobs. 'Yes. Injected the wrong dosage, wrong drug, used azeperone. Dong Zei started panicking almost immediately. Simon was able to stabilise her. They came to me together.' She sniffed. 'Simon kept talking about how it was essential that Ian not lose his reputation, legacy. That's what he kept saying.'

Catherine exhaled. 'So you agreed to an EEPV story, that Dong Zei had a virus?'

'It seemed harmless.'

'And you pocketed eighty grand and blamed Beau.'

'No.' Even in the dark cupboard Catherine could see her shake her head. 'There was no talk of blaming Beau. Simon ad-libbed that on the night of Dong Zei's death. I don't think even Ian knew.'

Catherine knelt down, fighting the urge to slap her. 'So, why let it go?'

'I didn't want to, but Beau was asking all the right questions. Simon's campaign against him seemed the best way to either discredit him, or silence him.' She kept on crying. 'I never knew he wouldn't–'

'Would you have let him keep his job?'

She nodded. 'All he had to do was be quiet. I'm not a monster.' Even in the cramped space, Catherine was disinclined to comfort the woman.

'Why take the money?'

Georgia kept crying, almost wailing. After a full minute, Catherine relented and held her. Georgia clung to her, continuing to cry. Catherine stroked her hair. The mystery was solved. Catherine thought of Britt and her gut flipped again. She rubbed her hand with the bloodied knuckles and thought about punching the door. It wouldn't help. She would just have to keep yelling.

'Hello? Help! Fire! Corruption! Hello?'

'Catherine.' A voice, outside.

'Hello, yes, help?'

'Catherine, are you in dis door?'

There was a knock on the metal. Urgent, but more gentle than a bullet. Dis door? African accent. Catherine's eyes opened wide in the cupboard. 'Philomena?'

'Yes, it's me. I'm sorry. I know you said you would prefer to be left alone.'

Catherine started jumping up and down. 'Quite acceptable under the circumstances. I'm going to push the key under the door.'

Boris shuffled against the wall. It was dark now that Simon had pulled the roller door back down. The cable ties Simon had used were tight. His hands were bound together under his thighs. Above him was some small viper's enclosure, emitting an eerie red light. Next to him, Britt was in the same predicament. A few metres in front of them, Simon was stroking the glass of the Philippines Crocodile. He had been doing that for the past few minutes. Britt was breathing deeply. Boris wondered if it were pain management. He was aware of nothing so much as his will to live and his smell.

'Forster.' Britt's voice was strong, not a quaver of fear. Boris couldn't help being surprised.

'What?' He didn't look away from the glass.

'They'll be here soon, Forster. Any chance of escape has gone.'

'Hostages,' he said half-heartedly.

'Buy you a few hours.'

'Yeah,' he said, almost nonchalantly. 'I wasn't going to escape anyway.' He turned around. 'It was all to protect his legacy, you understand. Now that's gone. He's gone, so I'm gone. All that's left is a little fun. It's really all one can ask for in life.'

He turned back to the glass. 'I always had such fun, with animals.'

Boris hadn't noticed the key in his hand, so when the glass opened, he swore, in a higher pitch than he would have liked.

Once outside, Catherine picked up her phone. The missed call was Boris. She rang it and talked to the bashful Philomena Kaboru while she waited for him to answer.

'I've been trying to call you.'

'I know. I was at a conference and I knew you had finished the hat. It was only when the conference finished an hour ago I suddenly knew I was in danger of not getting it. So I came here.'

Boris' phone rang out. Catherine swore, then looked back at Philomena. 'You're really single-minded, aren't you?'

Philomena drew herself tall. 'It's called goal-oriented.'

Georgia looked at them through tear-stained eyes. 'What are you talking about?'

Philomena looked at her haughtily. 'A most important hat.'

Catherine gazed westward. 'No time for this. Go call the police. Take Philomena with you.'

Philomena stepped forward. 'But the hat?'

'Is at my studio and will be gratis if I'm dead,' Catherine yelled over her shoulder. She ran in the general direction of the last bullet sound. It had come, she surmised, from the centre of the zoo. She ran south. As she passed the food court, she saw a grey gun on the path. Britt's. Catherine quickened her pace, her face set.

Britt had resisted her counsel, gone for the easy option and threatened to arrest Catherine but had fought like a lion under fire. She was a good friend and didn't deserve to die.

She came within sight of the southern exit and wondered where Simon would have taken her. If he had a car there was no knowing.

'Catherine.' A male voice yelled. Not Boris, slight brogue.

Andy waved her over to near the reptile house.

She made the ground in record time. 'What are you doing here? There's been a shooting?'

He was pale, eyes darting back to the reptile house. 'I heard. I was trying to get into the frogs when it started. Then I was stuck inside. I only got out a minute ago.'

'What?' The frog house was part of the reptile house, but had a separate door. The door was open. Catherine looked back at Andy.

He smiled bashfully. 'I think the keepers shut the place in a hurry.'

Catherine was looking for Britt, Simon, spots of blood. 'Have you heard anything else?'

'I thought I heard voices from in there.' He pointed to the closed roller doors of the reptile house. 'That's when I saw you.'

Catherine walked towards the doors. Andy grabbed her arm. 'What are you doing?'

She brushed his hand off. 'I know who's got the gun, and he's got a friend of mine in there.'

His hands were up, incredulous. 'You don't have a gun.'

Catherine shrugged. 'I have rhythm? Surely that's something, right?'

She moved towards the door, held her ear to it. She could hear voices, including high pitched swearing. She banged the door. 'Britt, are you in there?'

A voice she knew yelled an answer. 'Catherine, run!'

Catherine was astonished. 'Boris!'

Then a bullet came out of the iron and narrowly missed her head.

15

Half the world should have worried more, the other half less. The important thing is nobody was right. Carbon and regret are two certainties of human existence.

~ Molly O'Connor

Boris would have worried about wearing out the seat of his trousers, if he hadn't been so worried about the eyelash viper that seemed interested in him. Simon, once he started opening the viewing windows, systematically opened all of them. Snakes started slithering, tentatively, slowly and inexorably out of their cages and moving towards each other and the humans on the floor. Aside from this yellow slitherer, Boris was pleased to say that most of them seemed content to ignore him. The other good news was that he seemed to be able to go faster than the snakes simply by shuffling around on his bottom while his hands were tied under his thighs.

Britt was sitting dead still, her face an illuminated mask, her eyes following Boris. Simon was out of sight, probably making the full tour of the house, opening all the cages.

'Are you okay?' Boris asked Britt.

He couldn't remember if snakes were deaf or loved sound. He cursed himself for not paying attention in the lecture.

'I'm all right. I think staying still would be better for you. Aren't snakes attracted to movement?'

'I can't remember.' He paused. The viper came within a metre. He started moving again.

Britt grunted. 'Boris, can you get your hands under your arse?'

'What?'

'I'm watching your hands; you have long arms. You might be able to get them under your legs and be able to stand.'

'What about this snake?'

Her voice got higher. 'I don't think it matters.' Her expression turned horrified. Boris went stock still as a black snake about two metres long whipped past him and took the yellow viper in its jaws.

Boris made a wet sound, then pushed his wrists up over his backside. For a second he felt like his own arse would break his shoulders, but then he was able to get past his girth and his hands were behind his back. He shuffled to the nearest wall and was able to stand. He looked for something sharp to rub the cable tie with, could see nothing aside from things with teeth.

He looked at Britt. 'What now?'

'I don't know. Oh, shoot.' She inched away from a five metre python that was suddenly within cuddling range. Boris took two steps and kicked it away.

'This is intolerable,' he whispered.

They could hear Simon singing. Boris wasn't sure, but it sounded a lot like Depeche Mode.

'And getting worse,' whispered Britt.

'We have to wait for the police! Not even you're that mad!' Andy was beside himself as Catherine strode to the entrance of the frog house, looking at the roof.

'That's my best two friends in there. I have to do something.' She turned to him. 'What about the frog house? There's a connecting roof, isn't there?'

He looked uncomfortable, but nodded. 'Yes, I think so.'

'Good thing you left the door open. Great work.'

Andy made a high pitched sound.

Behind glass panels, lush nocturnal micro-environments held frogs from around the globe. Catherine ignored them. In a minute she spied the access hole against a corner of the low ceiling. 'Give me a boost?'

In four seconds, she was standing on his shoulders. In two minutes, she was in the roof. This was the good news, because she was on her belly surrounded by cables and air vents in the dark. She brought out her phone and switched the torch function on, then moved towards the right. It took a rate of a metre every minute, sliding over pipes that looked suspiciously like they carried either water or gas or both. Catherine wasn't keen on breaking them.

She listened for voices, heard a man singing about moths. Definitely not Boris. She moved away from the sound. Presently she came to another access hole. This one had a lock on it, but with two hair pins she had it open in seconds. She swung her head down, swearing quietly.

Underneath her, in the dark light, was a snake's tail, disappearing down the gullet of a very satisfied looking crocodile. Forster wasn't far off, watching the croc intently, not noticing Catherine.

She swung back into the roof and shut the access hole quietly, breathing very deeply in the dusty air. She moved a few more metres to the next hole, repeated the lock trick and swung her head down. Simon's singing waltzed around the tunnel of the reptile house. In the near distance were two figures, one standing and one sitting. She recognised their shapes.

'Boris,' she whispered.

He looked up. 'Catherine, what the hell are you doing?'

He turned and kicked a small adder off Britt's leg. It must have moved her ankle because Britt cried out in pain. Around the corner, the singing stopped and a peal of laughter floated towards them.

'Not long now,' Simon called out.

Boris was now underneath Catherine. 'What do you propose?'

'Remember that Swiss army knife you got me last Christmas?'

Boris smiled. 'Yeah?'

'Remind me to start carrying it.'

Boris' smile died.

In the roof, Catherine flashed her torch around her. It was cramped. There was the silver flash of air conditioning pipes, dusty cables and not much else. It was then she heard noise behind her and saw Andy scrambling up into the roof. Catherine grabbed an extension cord that was connecting a series of lights and pulled it, causing a crash about five metres away. She lowered the plug end down to Boris. 'Put that under your arms.'

Boris looked sceptical. 'How the hell are you going to lift me?'

'I've got back up.'

Boris made a show of looping it around himself and after thirteen seconds, had got absolutely nowhere. Catherine swung down and hit the floor with a thud. Gratefully, she could see no sign of the crocodile. In a second, she had it around his chest.

'What about Britt?' Boris whispered.

Catherine looked at her friend, tied up and unable to stand. 'We'll come back in a second.'

Britt whispered her two cents worth. 'What the hell would you do anyway, Boris? Break my other ankle? Go get the cavalry.'

The sound of Simon singing came closer. Catherine practically ran up Boris' body and leapt up to the low roof, the cord in her teeth. Once inside she threw the end to Andy and helped him pull.

It was a huge strain, even had they been standing, Boris was a decent ninety kilos and the cord stretched in their hands. The singing got louder. Catherine's arms were about to give way just as Boris' head came above the line of the roof. He used his chin to help the ascent. Once his shoulders were in, Catherine grabbed him, bending a pipe underneath her and pulling with everything she had.

As they shut the access hole, Britt's phone started to chime.

Catherine used the hairpins to weaken and break the cable ties, after which Boris was able to follow Andy back to the access hole that took them to the safety of the frog house. Boris needed more help than usual getting down from the roof. Catherine could see he was exhausted.

As Catherine landed she saw Andy quietly vomiting in the corner of the frog house and heard the yelling outside.

She hugged Boris, burying her face in his shoulder.

'Ow,' he said, wincing. 'My back isn't going to heal at all if we keep doing this.'

'You okay?'

He nodded, gulping in huge breaths of air. 'Yep. Don't ever buy me a snake.'

Catherine sobbed, just once. 'You stink, dear.'

A tear ran down his face. 'And I was just about to thank you for saving me.'

Andy brought his head up and wiped his mouth. 'Christ, don't mention it.'

Darkness had fallen when they went outside, but the lights were on. Catherine was disappointed to find not a police critical response unit but four uniforms, a few keepers and Kenneth Williams. His shoulders sagged when he saw them.

'What the hell are you doing here?'

Catherine half snarled and half smiled. 'Being proved right.'

'Where's Houden?'

Boris came forward. 'She's in there with a broken ankle. Simon Forster is armed. He's let all the snakes free.'

Williams stared for one second, then his face flickered. 'Forster broke her ankle?'

Boris shook his head. 'I did.'

'I should have guessed. What does Forster want?'

'He's flipped. Says he wants fun. There's snakes everywhere.'

Catherine chimed in. 'You know Forster has shot Bradbury?'

'Yes, I'm up with that.'

'Just checking.'

'Right.' Williams pointed at the uniforms. 'You blokes, we can't wait for the criticals, get your guns ready.' He pointed to the keepers. 'You blokes, stay back, but be ready to catch some snakes.'

A keeper came forward. 'We have to secure the outside area or we could risk losing the animals.'

Williams turned to him. 'Do I look like I give a rat's? Get ready.' He looked at Boris and Catherine. 'Which side is she?'

Boris pointed left. 'About ten metres that way.'

He shook his head. 'Christ.'

Williams moved to the side of the door, motioned for people to get out of range. He banged it twice.

'Simon Forster!'

He banged it again. Catherine knew he was counting to three. He shot the door lock, opened it and ran in. Alone.

They heard two shots. It was over in seconds.

16

Never smile at a crocodile – song written by Churchill/Lawrence.
~ Occasionally whistled by Kenneth Williams

Forty minutes later, Britt finally let the ambulance take her away. She had insisted on waiting until all the reptiles had been accounted for. The keepers, despite their initial protests, had been fantastic. Amazingly, there were only the three casualties. One eyelash viper, taken by a python. One black lipped cobra, taken by a big Philippine crocodile, and Simon Forster who was taken by the same croc just as he fired on Williams. The croc taking his leg had meant he missed Williams.

Williams hadn't missed, but was happy for the croc to take the credit. It was the first time he had fired his weapon in a thirty-five-year career.

Williams had, for his trouble, been bitten by an adder, and so accompanied Britt back to the Royal Melbourne for treatment. Catherine would later blame the venom of the adder for the choice words with which Williams "debriefed" the two of them prior to his departure in an ambulance.

'Have you ever been sworn at so much in your life?' Catherine asked Boris.

'No.' His phone rang. 'I think I'm about to be, though.' He turned away. 'Hi Molly.'

Catherine left him to it. She saw Georgia handing her passport over to a uniform. Andy came over, covered in a police blanket.

'So, drink?'

'I think you've earned one.'

He chewed some gum and looked at the reptile house. 'I couldn't believe we got the big bugger into the roof.'

'Oh, he's losing weight. He's vegetarian, you know.'

Days later, Catherine, Boris, Molly and Andy were in that suburban Garden of Eden, the beer garden of the Glasgow Palace.

'So why did she take the money?' Molly, whose initial fury had subsided once she realised Catherine had saved Boris this time, was playing catch-up with the case.

Catherine finished her drink and picked up a fresh glass off the table. 'Georgia, it turns out, had a weak spot for the pokies. When Bradbury and Forster came to her, she saw that there was no saving the elephant, but there was a chance to save her mortgage. She took the cash, they agreed to hush it up. Then Simon wanted the extra of Beau taking the fall, and started orchestrating the staff against Beau. When that didn't work, he made sure the dogs finished him off. He must have pulled some serious gymnast moves to get away cleanly before Bradbury saved Beau.'

Boris chimed in. 'So you're sure Bradbury wasn't involved?'

'I don't think so,' Catherine said. 'He was a wonderful man who made mistakes. He deserves a half great legacy.'

Molly burped quietly 'So much pain, just for money.'

'Tell me about it,' said Andy, 'I've been queasy ever since.'

Catherine rolled her eyes. Someone put the outdoor heater on, Catherine sank back into its warmth, and felt alive.

Boris accompanied her to Bradbury's funeral. It was a huge ceremony with many dignitaries and televised for a worldwide audience. Fans, family and friends heard the story of a man who had followed his passion, sometimes at the cost of his family. Catherine saw a woman her own age, who nodded when the preacher spoke of Ian's only grandchild, Rachel. Later, the same woman comforted a man in his fifties who cried bitterly as Ian's tributes were read out.

Catherine took Boris' hand in hers, and looked at the coffin that held the body of a decent man, whose reputation was safe. She remembered another coffin that held a great man, whose reputation was now also safe.

Occasionally Catherine was distracted by the sight of a green hat. A hat whose haughty wearer would never know about the hidden strand of cotton sewn into it. Khaki cotton from the discarded sock of a loving zoo-keeper. Stained with dried elephant dung.

Catherine knew you're not supposed to smile at a funeral, but today that was hard work.

ACKNOWLEDGEMENTS

I'm hugely grateful to Lindy Cameron from Clan Destine Press for bringing this book back into print. Also to Narrelle Harris who gave it a once over with her eagle editor eyes and fierce brain.

The below acknowledgements were written three years ago. The comments are as relevant today as they were then.

Hats off, as ever, to the wonderful Annie Hall, publisher, editor and constant support. Annie's commitment to her authors and their characters means that you are holding a much stronger story for the extra year it took to write. It's a relationship I cherish, not least for the fact that all assertions must be researched and correct, yet I'm allowed to add a psychic character without her batting an eyelid.

The research for this book ranged from vegetarianism to millinery fashion to elephant husbandry. I was hugely helped regarding elephants by my dear friend Dr Emily Treweek, who both researched and guided my own in a very strange assignment that took her away from her usual role as a vet. In a lovely synergy, Em's husband Dusty – chef extraordinaire – gave excellent pointers on vegetarianism.

My medical research was pushed along nicely by my brilliant and medical in-laws: Alexandra Kent and Hans Hollorer. Alex read through my scenes in ICU and was generously on call for medicine 101 questions. Hans gave invaluable insight into the nature of infections and just how much fun they can be – theoretically.

June Edwards remains my millinery contact, striving for a fairer world and fashion brilliance simultaneously.

Agent K in CSI keeps me up to date with the Crime Scene world and technology used within.

The wonderful Debbie Rowland was a welcome sight at many of my Zoo jaunts. Deb was a great friend to make for her Zoo stories, general knowledge and connections to the best sushi in the place.

Then comes the writing, which was hugely helped by feedback from Michael Hearn and Kate Sandford. Michael discussed tonality, pitch and timing, sometimes pushing, sometimes challenging, always hitting the mark and vastly improving the work.

Kate, who is brilliant and brutal in equal measure, gave hours of her time gratis and closed the door on a plot line that was never going to work (hindsight and all that), if only your best friends will tell you the bad news, Kate is the best you can get.

Belated thanks to Charles Horvath, who delivered similar bad news when I was at the last stages of writing Jinx and who was never acknowledged publicly.

The people I live with are wonderful. A real turning point in the writing came when my daughter Eliza, aged seven, sat beside me for a session and laughed at jokes in real time. Her brother Cormac was always up for a chat about my story and has a laugh that should be bottled. Both the kids were great company in the several field trips I made to the Zoo during the research for this book, which was an unabashed mix of business and pleasure.

Louise, my wife, is the most amusing of muses, sharpest of wits and the best person to sit on a couch with at the end of a long day.

Those long days were made easier by the countless folk who enjoyed Jinx and took the time to tell me so. Being regularly told 'I'm waiting for the next one, please get on with it' is the sincerest and most appreciated form of encouragement.

An affectionate nod to my parents, Andrea and Hugh, who are proud that I'm an author, but were proud of me when I washed dishes for a living too, that matters.

When it seemed this project would get the better of me, I was supported and inspired by Patrick Northey, who was also writing a book about elephants and who helped me restructure the manuscript. Patrick's death in August 2016 was unexpected and tragic, leaving many projects unfinished, a family heartbroken and a community devastated. The dedication page is a small tribute to a creative powerhouse and a great man.

AUTHOR'S NOTE

This is a work o fiction based in a real place. Melbourne Zoo is real. The dysfunction and dastardly deeds in this book are figments of my imagination. Having been to the zoo a couple of billion times as "research" (also known as "having somewhere to take the children") I can say that I have never seen it as anything but a well-run, not-for-profit workplace, where animals and staseem quite happy. The chips are a bit pricey, but I shan't let that tarnish a great organisation.

HUGH McGINLAY

Hugh is a writer and musician. These poor career choices means that he has also worked as a bus driver, a kitchenhand, singing teacher and a seller of dental consumables. He loves lying in hammocks, rereading books and walking around airports holding a guitar case. He lives in Melbourne with his wife Louise, their two children, a cat and six chickens.